the Moon Within

Aida Salazar

SCHOLASTIC INC.

"This is a fascinating tale that blends ancestral traditions from two cultures, while portraying modern dilemmas. Salazar's poetry is as lovely and graceful as the dance scenes." —**Margarita Engle, National Young People's Poet Laureate and Newbery Honor-winning author of** *The Surrender Tree*

"With conga-pulsed lyrics, Aida Salazar pulls us into the coming of age of eleven year Celi. She initiates readers into the conversation of Bomba, the girl-woman circle, divine twin energies and the many moon-tide powers of a Latina pre-teen. This is a book whose form and content, vision and depth, I find revolutionary and culturally ecstatic. In these times, here is the liberation verse our youth and all have been waiting for—Brava-Bravo!" —**Juan Felipe Herrera, former US Poet Laureate and author of** *Jabberwalking*

"Aida Salazar has reached deep into our indigenous past to explore in beautiful, poignant poetry what it means to become a woman at the intersection of community and self. Rooted in ancestral lore yet vibrantly modern, *The Moon Within* is a touching, powerful, and important novel in verse." —**David Bowles, Pura Belpré Honor-winning author of** *The Smoking Mirror*

"In a vivid, magical debut, Aida Salazar's lyrical poetry deftly pulls you into Celi's vibrant world as she reluctantly dances towards womanhood, adjusting to the drumbeats of first love and true friendship while exploring her ancestral roots as she finds her role within family and community." —**Naheed H. Senzai, award-winning author of** *Shooting Kabul* **and** *Escape from Aleppo*

"Lovely and amazing . . . a heartbreaker, in every wonderful way. Salazar's vivid and accessible verse brings us the coming-of-age story we've been longing for. Poignant, funny, and deeply moving, *The Moon Within* is a story told with an abundance of love and respect—a gift straight from the center of Salazar's heart to readers everywhere." —**Olugbemisola Rhuday-Perkovich, author of** *Eighth-Grade Superzero* **and co-author of** *Naomis Too*

NEW MOON

○

"We are all like the bright moon,
we still have our darker side."

— Kahlil Gibran

To Avelina, Amaly, João and John,
the moons and stars in the
universe de mi corazón.

To all girls and xochihuah,
may this flower song lift you
with radical love and resistance.

"The moon reaches her zenith—
Her glow silvering the world.
Joy sings out
Within every good soul."
—"A Flower Song for Maidens
Coming of Age" from
Songs of Dzitbalché 7,
translated by David Bowles

Text copyright © 2019 by Aida Salazar
Illustrations copyright © 2019 by Joe Cepeda

This book was originally published by Arthur A. Levine Books,
an imprint of Scholastic Inc., in 2019.

ISBN 978-1-338-28338-9

10 9 8 7 6 5 4 3 2   21 22 23 24

Printed in the U.S.A. 40
This edition first printing 2020

Book design by Maeve Norton

The text was set in ITC Legacy Serif Std Book,
with display type set in AgedBook Regular.

"A Flower Song for Maidens Coming of Age"
printed with permission from David Bowles

MY LOCKET

There is a locket in my heart → Metaphor
that holds all of the questions → ignor
that do cartwheels in my mind
and gurgle up to the top of my brain
like root beer fizz. → Simile

Questions that my journal
doesn't keep so my little brother, Juju,
or other snoops don't read them.
Questions that Mima
knows how to answer
but I'm too embarrassed to ask her
because they might
seem stupid   or gross   or wrong.

Like, why have my armpits begun to smell?
Or how big will my breasts grow?
Or when exactly will my period come?

I flush bright red

right through my amber skin
just thinking about it.

It was so long ago that Mima was
eleven, maybe she wouldn't
remember what it is like
maybe she'll make me talk about it, a lot
maybe wind herself into a lecture
about the beauty of women's bodies
that I don't want to hear from her
sometimes cactus lips.
Maybe she'll just think I'm
delirious and say,
Celi, are you running a fever?
while she kisses my forehead.

My locket also keeps secrets.

Secrets tangle in the shyness of my tongue
even when I try to tell them
to my best friend
Magda.

Instead, my locket holds quiet my crush
on Iván who is one year older
than me and who can do a backflip
better than the other boys in his capoeira class.

Or the wish that Aurora, my "friend"
would just go away and
not have a crush on him too.
Or how often I sneak the tablet
from my parents when
I'm supposed to be practicing
music or dancing.

Though I've never seen it
I know my locket is there.
It keeps my questions
          my secrets
warm
unanswered
and safe.

LUNA

A beam of moonlight
squeezes through
my window's curtain.

Luna is out tonight.

My eyes wide open like doors. *Simile*

I'll be twelve in a few months, I should
be allowed to go to sleep later
than seven-year-old Juju, who shares a room with me
        but I'm not.
        No matter that it is Saturday.
Round-cheeked Juju passes
out the moment his head hits the pillow.

And I stare at the May moonlight.

I watch her light up a sliver of dust
in my room.

Like a performance   ➤ *Simile*
small specks dance
twirl,

      bounce,

               float,

    glide,

        somersault.

They dance like I do.

I try to memorize their choreography
to use during bomba dance class
when Magda drums for me
and I am free to improvise
bring my own moves.

I smile to think that specks of dust
    dance around me   ➤ *personification*
though I don't hear music.
Maybe they dance to the clicks and creaks
of our little house in Oakland
    and the city crickets
      and Mima's and Papi's footsteps
        outside my door
          Juju's steady breathing.

And when Luna is gone
and I can't see their floating
I know they continue to dance
in a dream
with Luna and me.

MOON CEREMONY

Mima says judging by my body
that soon my moon will come
and with it
my moon ceremony.
It's a period, Mima, I tell her, not a moon.
She whips back,
It will come every twenty-nine days
just like the moon.
So it's a moon cycle.

She doesn't know that the moon
is a dancer to me, not a period.

I dread the ceremony where she will gather
all six of my aunts
some of my dance teachers
a constellation of grown-up women
to talk to me
about what it means to bleed monthly
and worse, I'll have to openly share
my body's secret

my locket's secret
as if on display
like a ripe mango on a fruit stand. *Simile*
I just about lose my lunch and I can't
roll my eyes back into my head anymore.

Mima tosses her long night-black hair
to the side to explain for the twentieth time
while I turn my back and imitate her words:
Our ancestors honored
our flowering in this way.
It is a ritual taken away from us
during so many conquests.

The thought of having to talk
to anyone
especially adults
about secrets only meant for my
locket makes my insides crumble,
I won't do it!
Please, Mima, please don't make me do it.
Embarrassment will eat me up whole!
I shout from my heart.

Don't worry, Celi, she calms,
your body will tell us when it is time.

NAILS

Long and thick and
painted bright red
is how I dream
they could be.
But they are
little nubs at my fingertips
small, gnarled, and crusty.

I bite them and don't
think about it like when you
eat popcorn during a movie.
I do it mostly when I listen
to Magda tell me a story
or when Iván is around
and I pretend not to stare.

Mostly it's a nervous habit
like anxious ants crawling inside my fingertips.
My parents and my dance teacher, Ms. Susana, all say,
Celi, stop biting your nails!

But soon, up they zoom, right to my mouth
when I'm learning new choreography
or waiting for my turn to dance.

Mima says I can't paint them
red until after I'm thirteen
officially a teenager
which makes me growl
at her under my breath.
Plus, she talks about bacteria
that lingers in your fingers
and though it grosses me out
I easily forget and I'm picking
at the little bits of skin
that hang from my cuticles.

Dr. Guillermo, my dentist,
said to put a bunch of sticky notes
around my house or in my books
to remind me to stop biting.
That's how he gets his patients to
stop grinding their teeth.
I do it for a week but it's no use.

I can't explain it
biting my nails

brings me a comfort like
drinking hot chocolate
or eating warm handmade tortillas
for breakfast.

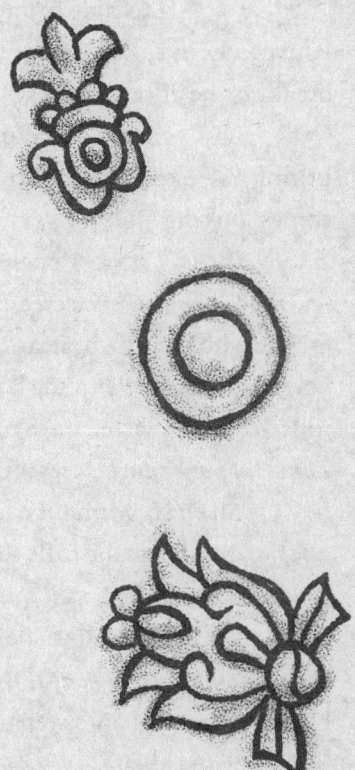

A CLOSET FULL

Monday morning before school, I can't change
in our only bathroom, Mima's in there
       so I squeeze into the closet
          to hide from Juju.
Papi comes in to call me for the
breakfast he always makes
          but I stay quiet cool
I think I've escaped but soon Mima
comes looking and
            opens the door
Ay, mija, I love it! she screams
for the whole house to hear.
I clutch at the new bra she bought me
roller-coaster twisted onto my chest.
The straps are tangled, let me fix it.
      Sh sh sh, Mima! I whisper hard.
As she untangles, she calls for Papi,
Amor! Come see how well this bra fits Celi!
She shakes her head like she doesn't believe it,
It's amazing, just look at this muchachita, está floreciendo.
I hear Juju's and Papi's steps approach

their footfalls, a growing heated
pounding in my head.
I contort into a pretzel
inside that
shrinking
closet,

>   Mima! No!
Quieta, there's nothing to be ashamed of, Celi —
*   it's cause for celebration!*
What? What's a celebration? Papi asks.
Breasts, our girl is growing breasts!

> [handwritten: I am so glad our parents don't do that to me!]

Mima's high pitch sears my ears.
Awesome! Juju chimes in.
When I'm eleven, will I grow some too?
>   Shut up! You little . . . I strike.
Celi, Papi warns, but then turns to Juju,
It isn't likely, mijo. They're mammary glands designed
to nurse young. Remember, like the mama goats we saw?
You mean, like goat teats? Juju cracks up
lets out his annoyingly loud goat bleat,
Celi's got teats!
My skin swells with an out-of-control fire,
>   MIMA! I cry, as helpless as ash.
She hugs me so tight and kisses me
all over my sizzling face and head.
I'm just so thrilled for you, Celi. It really is a marvelous moment.
I jerk away and turn my back on all three of them

slip on my top, wishing to disappear into a flame.
When I turn around, Mima's got tears in her eyes!
Vamos, Papi hugs and nudges her and Juju away,
Let's give Celi some privacy.

I burst from that cramped space
breathing a burning anger in and out of my lungs.
My fiery eyes land on the picture
of my family and me in front of my
eleventh birthday cake and I take
scissors to their smiling faces
and mine
until
we
are in
a
million
pieces
like
my
locket.

PUFFER BRA

At school
      I am a puffer fish
slick new bra glistening
          beneath my blouse
harmless
          to those who don't know
          or don't care what I wear
     ever
     like Magda
but chest expanded dangerous
     to the first kid to dare ask,
Is that a bra strap I see?

OAKLAND ORANGE SKY

After school, I walk seven steps ahead of Mima and Juju
to my ballet class at the Oakland Ballet Conservatory
only a few blocks from my house.
As my legs grow longer
my strides cover more ground.
I can't be late or I'll lose my scholarship.

Oakland
     b
         r
            e
                a
                   k
                     s

open before me
the sun sets brightly in this almost summer
it unfurls an orange-gray glaze over the city.

I pretend like I'm on my own.

Soon I'll be able to walk to class
            without Mima.
What could go wrong in three blocks?
For now, the wind brushes my curls
I can smell the exhaust of cars
mixed with the smell of sour grass
broken after mowing.
I pass a pile of baby gear
sitting on the curb with a sign
that says Free on it.
I slap at blades of foxtail shoots
and gather their feathery tufts
as I walk.

The man with the long ponytail
who's always home
stands outside his house smoking
and his pit bull sits on the steps, off leash.
I hold my breath and slow my stride.
I don't want the dog to come chasing.

I make a left on MacArthur
to find a tangerine sky
turn back to see
if Mima is still
behind
me.

I'm relieved that she is
because there are kids on MacArthur
getting loud with each other.

They gather at a bus stop
in their school uniforms
a flock of crows waiting to get home.
A teenage girl starts a fight with a boy
she swings her arms at him
while he walks backward into the street
and everyone's screaming
        phones are out.
I can't tell if they are playing or for real
so, I slow down completely and grab Mima's arm.
        A bitter citrus cielo draped over us.
Then suddenly, they are all laughing
and cursing like nothing happened.

I wonder why they joke like that
and why they aren't going
to a dance class like me.

LIKE A REDWOOD

On Thursday, I wait to see him
walk into La Peña Cultural Center.
Iván of the shy smile
light-bark-brown skin
dark bushy curls on top
that shape into a peak
like a growing tree.
Branch-like legs
and arms so lanky long
they reach for the sun
when he plays capoeira.

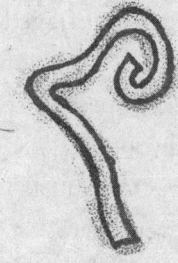

I look for him in the studio's big mirror
during my own dance class
talking to his friends
his gym bag strapped across his back
his skateboard in one hand.
He waits for my bomba class
to end and file out
and his capoeira class to begin.

He only waves, maybe says *hi*
every Thursday, no more and no less.

He seems to be getting to the other
side of growing up with that crackle in his voice
and the bumps sprawled on his forehead.

I pretend to gather my things slowly
my eyes strain to sideways stalk him.
In his class, he sways — a ginga —
his hands up, ready, like a boxer
graceful in that martial art
of fighting camouflaged by dance.

Last summer, we went to arts camp together
in the Redwoods
as far from Oakland as I go alone.
When we were there
we'd talk during lunch.
Once he told me he lived
with his mom and that his pop
wasn't around much and that
even though he's not Brazilian
playing capoeira helps him
keep his mind off missing his pop.

I opened my locket

a little too to say
though I'm half Puerto Rican
dancing bomba feels
like warm Caribbean water
swishing and swaying
happiness inside of me.
Which made him grin giggle
and made me want to bury
my blushing head in the dirt.

Though we are away from the forest now
I like to hear him say
hello in that broken way
that he does sometimes
and remember the smell of redwoods
and us together
for just a second.

MY BEST ECHO

Magda is better than my best friend
strange maybe
because we aren't anything alike.
I wear my curly hair
cola de caballo long
or pulled back in a bun
and love the flowing cotton skirts
girls have to wear to dance bomba.
She wears her bright brown hair
short
T-shirt, jeans, and high-top Vans
skater boy style
and hardly dances.
She only drums.

She is a smaller
eleven-year-old than others
maybe because her growing
hasn't kicked in yet.
But the power in her hands is so big
the sound bounces off the drum

fills the room
and sinks into your bones.
She's by far the best drummer in our
bomba performance group, Farolitos,
and the best at smiling.
Magda knows how to work up
the crowd at shows
with a quick flash
of her wide white teeth.

I think I dance the best
when she drums.
When I make a move
and mark it with my twirling skirt, a piquete,
she hits the drum right at that moment.
Like an echo, but better because it's as if
she can read my mind and finds
my next move before I do.

She is my best echo.

BOYNESS

Before our last performance
a couple of weeks ago
Magda waited for one of the
bathroom stalls to be free.
Auburn-haired Aurora says,
You can't really be in the girls' bathroom.
Magda chuckles back. *Course I can. I'm a girl.*
She knew what Aurora was hinting at
because others often asked her
about how much boyness
she had versus girlness.

Mima was in the bathroom too
brushing my hair into a tight bun
that stretched my eyes
like rubber bands
and we quietly looked on.

Aurora raised her screechy voice and blurted,
*My mom says you hate yourself and that's
why you want to be a boy.*

Magda flushed red
to the tips of her ears.
She turned her back to Aurora
rubbed her hands in her face
as if to stop tears from coming
all of us stood silenced, in shock.

Wait a minute, Aurora!
Mima lets my hair go
and marches over to the girls.
Magda has more love for herself
than any of us.
She knows herself so well
she can be anyone she wants.
And you can tell your mami
I said that.

It was a good thing Mima was there.
Thoughts stalled in my mind
like a broken-down car
but my uneasy thoughts
wanted to drive off
and think of happy things
like how fun it is
for Magda and me
to learn to ride skateboards
        or

hold our tongues so that normal words
sound like bad words
      or
play echo when we perform.

Magda smiled big
grabbed Aurora and hugged
her with one arm
gave her a little nudge
on the head as if to say,
You booger — knock it off.

TWO-THREE PULSE

I looked to Magda
when we were alone
in the bathroom.
Scanned her
for what she must be feeling.
The right words blocked in my boca
by my bitten nails.
Couldn't describe how bad I felt
for having stayed quiet
for letting Mima speak for her
for not knowing how to
defend her from Aurora la rudeness
who has chisme caught in every breath.
Of all people, Aurora, whose light skin
makes that big brown mole
at her temple look
like it's a third eye
and who squeals each time
she sees Iván like some loca.

I found Magda's two dark brows

lifting like umbrellas
Oh, I just learned this hambone
two-three rhythm like in clave.
You wanna learn?
I squeaked,
      You okay, Magda?
She didn't answer, instead
she grabbed my hands, and our
eyes locked like a pinky swear
in a never-mind-Aurora kind of way.
We both grinned like two weirdos
each ounce of discomfort
smacked away
in a hand-warming hambone

two
          then three
then two
          then three
               pulse . . .

MIMA'S HERBS

Mima says yerbitas can heal us.
Drunk or eaten herbs
can cure what bugs you:
fever, sniffles, headache, nerves,
cramps, bellyache, toothaches,
and growing pains.

She learned this from her mother, Yeya,
who learned it from her mother
who learned it from her mother
like that
      all
         the
            way
               down
a long line of herbal women in Mexico
      and she teaches me too.

She grows them
in the garden.
Sometimes in little pots out back.

This is how I love them best
so I pick at them
with the tips of my
nail-less fingers.
Snap a tender twig
right from the plant
and eat it in the sun.

I watch Mima make tinctures
strong teas, and salves
for friends and clients who are sick.
Funny thing, they do get better.

She got rid of my
molluscum contagiosum — warts on my chin and feet —
by smothering each wart
with dragon's blood — a stinky red sap
from a Mexican tree
that smells like a cross
between feet and barf.

She gave Luis, Magda's dad,
a tea so strong, it stopped
his flaming bowel from making
him fold over in pain.

Tonight, I'm working on a list of all the herbs

I know and what they're good for
and typing them right into my tablet
in case I can use it for a science report:
>Yerba Buena — bellyache and foggy brain
>Arnica — bruises and sprains
>Rosemary — poor eyesight and dandruff
>Lemon Balm — jumpy nerves and cold sores
>Manzanilla — bellyache and insomnia
>Dragon's Blood — warts, moles, acne, and other wild
>bumps

Maybe one day, aside from a dancer
I'll be an herbalist too.

MY FLOWER,
MI FLOR

Flor is the name Mima
has called my down-there girl parts
since I was very little
when she taught me to wash myself.
She held a mirror between my legs
let me inspect between the petals
and ask questions:
Why does it look like that?
Why is this button here
and opening there?

*This little one here is for your pee — remember to wipe front to
back to keep it healthy.*
*This one here is your birth canal — the place where babies pass as
they are born — which leads to the uterus where they grow.*
*And this button here is only for you — it's your happy button. You
get to choose when to push it.*
*Our flores are women's most magical parts, mija. Aren't we
lucky?*

I didn't think too much
about it all back then
and am only sometimes reminded
when I feel a sparkly tickle in my flor
when we go down a big hill
or I'm on a carnival ride.

Lately, the tingle happens
when I think of Iván.
Butterflies flutter first in my panza
and then they make their way down

        in a

        trickle

        to

        my

         flor.

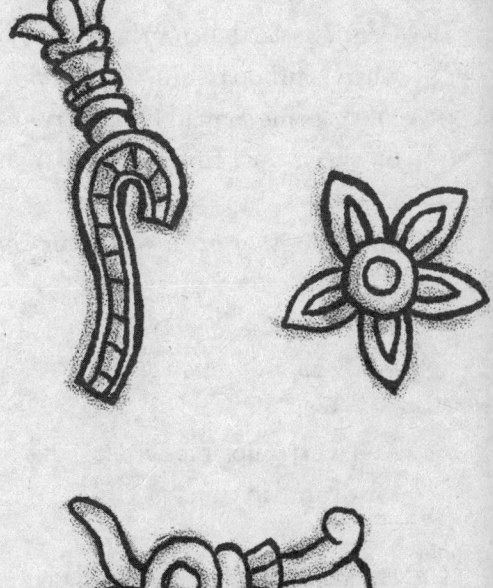

I wonder if anyone can tell
that my flor is sparkling?

But then I remember
what Mima said,
It's only for me.
I'm relieved that
nobody can.

PAPA DRUM

My father is a drum.
Big barrel chest
that he uses to practice the rhythms
of his congas when he's not near them
where a big barrel voice pops out
when he sings or yells for me to come.

Gentle as earth beneath my feet
when I curl up to him when
Juju gets me so mad I could cry
or when I can't find the drum in me.
He says,
Sing from your breath and from your heart.

Kae, Kae, Kae, Yemayá olodo
Kae, Kae, Kae, asesú olodo

And when I do, it is better.
My drum's in tune.

Hands so rough and calloused

you'd think he pounded nails
for a living but he is
a conguero.
His living is music.
Percussive pak, pok, dum, dim
fills our house daily.
Probably why I came out
dancing.
From the start
Mima's heartbeat
Papa Drum's music
like my soundtrack
and so I dance and sing along.

PAPER WALLS

Up late on a Saturday night.
Juju sleeps.
Luna wanes.

The dancers come into
our room again
not dressed as brightly.

As I watch them pirouette
I can hear Mima and Papi
speaking in the dining room
outside our bedroom.

Their voices vibrate
harmonica-like
through paper walls.
I can tell it is something
intense because of the
singsong way that their
voices climb and fall
whisper and punch

and I tune in. . . .

Mima, please slow down with her. She's too young to be dealing with all of this grown women's stuff.

> *Are you blind, amor? Haven't you seen how her body is developing?*

You should be encouraging her to be a better artist, a better dancer, a better student, not a grown woman.

> *She can be all those things and still celebrate the healthy development of her body.*

I guess I just don't want my little girl to go. Can't you let her come to it on her own and not because you want it a certain way?

> *Her changes are going to happen whether we like it or not. Es la ley de la vida.*

But don't you think she needs her privacy? A little space?

> *Yes, but she can only get so much when she and Juju are crammed into that room.*

I mean from you and this moon ceremony.

*From me? Wait one second, amor. I'll be damned if MY
daughter comes into her womanhood in ignorance of her
body and her connection to the universe.*

But she's just a little girl, Mima.

*Yes, a BLOSSOMING little girl who is almost twelve and
very soon will be a woman. She is going to need all of her
power, all of her self-knowledge, and all of her community
when it comes.*

I hear a bang
like someone slammed the dining room table
and I can't tell if it's Mima or Papi.
I hear scrambling and complaints about
a glass of spilled water.
Then they are quiet.

Though I wish Mima
would listen to Papi
I wonder what all of my power looks like
and how much of me there is left to know.

JUJU BOLT

Juju was born
     with a broken heart
          and blue eyes.

He came the night of a big storm
so tiny he looked brittle
and was sort of ugly.

Mima said he looked
like a baby bird who'd fallen from its nest
or more like a viejito ruso, a Russian old man
with his white skin, bald head, and light eyes.

No one could explain exactly why
he was so fair, so unlike
the bronze of our skin
except for Mima, who said that
five hundred years of colonization
gave him those colors
and that he would brown up in no time.

And he has, though that was never the worry.

The doctors said only
open-heart surgery could repair
his tetralogy of Fallot — a heart br o k en

                 in
                 four
                 places.

Mima cried so much
partly because her herbs
couldn't fix him
mostly because there was a risk
that he could die on the table.

But he didn't.
He came back like a
little bolt of lightning.

I would sing songs to him
to stop him from crying
and because Papi says
that music can heal us too.

I like to think that it worked
because now his heart is all sealed.

He is as dorado as me
though still has those crazy blue eyes
     and his mouth moves faster than
          any lightning strike could ever catch.

PIECES OF US

Sunday morning
I come into our bedroom after breakfast.
Mima's got the trash can turned upside down
and everything's scattered on the floor
like fallen flower petals on the ground.
She and Juju search for something
like they often do for his lost Lego pieces
but this time, Mima is crying quietly.

        What'd you break now, Juju? I begin to scold
but she looks up and freezes my words
with a cold how-could-you look.
Then I see that she's got the tiny
pieces of our faces in her palm —
our eyes and smiles,
hair, bodies,
my eleventh birthday cake —
cut into strange triangles,
wonky squares, and rhombuses.
I didn't think you hated us so much, mija?
Then *I* begin to tear apart
to see Mima so upset because

of my moment of flaming coraje.
I manage to tremble quietly,
      I was just mad.
At what, Celi? What did we ever do?
I can't bring myself to tell her
what I really want to say at first.
Answer me, Celi — qué?
I close my eyes
too heavy with tears now
and the words stumble from me:
      I don't want to share
      what happens to my body
      with the whole world!
      It's nobody's business.
      You have no right, Mima.
      It's *my* body!
I crack open my eyes
to see a gash of hurt rip across
the onyx of her wet eyes,
But, mija, you should have nothing to hide
from Papi and Juju and me.
It is   a   beautiful   thing,   what's
happening   to   you.
She mutters sweetly with lots of spaces
between each word, which collide inside of me.
She comes to hold me
but I push away.

Juju's mouth drops open
and Mima's pierced heart
drains the softness from her cry.
Her weep deepens
but I don't care.

Mima kneels down
picks up a piece of the torn photo —
it's half of *her* face — and shows it to me,
We are a family, Celi. You came from my blood.
There is no use in trying to cut us out or push me away
because nothing will ever change that.
She begins to move toward the door
but swoops up my tablet
and takes it with her.
I fling myself
onto my bed and

                        scream

into my pillow.
I feel a Lego piece
        hit
my back
when Juju leaves
to go look for Mima.

BLACK-XICAN

Magda catches me hiding as I watch Iván
do skateboard tricks outside La Peña.
Luckily Aurora the pest is not around
drooling all over him.
So Magda settles next to me
to follow him as
he swishes
                glides
      skips
scratches up the concrete planter.

Iván is Black-xican — Black and Mexican
        mixed like me.
A little different than my
Black-Puerto Rican-Mexican-ness
but with the exact same deep amber in our skin
and reddish-brown honey in our eyes.

Painted on the underside of his skateboard deck
is an Aztec calendar on one end
and a Black Panther on the other.

We hear him tell his friend
that he and his Mexican dad
painted that board
       together
before his dad left.

MAMA EARTHS

Mima and Magda's mom, Teresa,
sit and talk in La Peña's café
while they wait for our bomba class to end.
They are friends since college
from their Xicana Power organizing days
when they started to learn about being Mexica
about our Aztec ancestors
and lost history.

Teresa's a chiropractor
easy harmony with herbalist Mima.
They reconnected when they went for
their doctorate degrees at NCHU—
Northern California Holistic University—
while pregnant with us and studying in their fields.
They've brought Magda and me together
since we were babies.

Now they're
Dr. Teresa Sánchez and Dr. Amelia Rivera
though Magda and I call them

Dr. Fixabones and Dr. Potions.
They are in the same women's circle
a place where they meet monthly
to dream, create art, talk or cry,
drink tea or wine or whatever.
It's my monthly stress relief, Mima says.

I secretly hate the women's circle.
That's where she got
the moon ceremony idea
in the first place.

I suspect some of those women
are coming to this moon ceremony
if I have it.

IF . . .

Little do they know
Luna cares more about dancing
than menstruation.

MAGDA'S DRUM LOCKET

Papi teaches our world drums
and songs class
on Tuesday afternoons at La Peña.

Magda sits close
I make funny eyes at her
so she laughs
but she shakes her head
turns up one edge of her lips
shows only half a dimple
and locks her focus on Papi
who the kids call Mr. Rivera.

He talks about how much we
owe our ancestors for music
and that the drum is like
a lifeline to community
and makes every bit of us strong.
      Magda takes his words down deep.

Perhaps she has her own drum locket
where she stores all she secretly loves too?

Pride folds over her
and drops to the light drumming
of her fingers on her lap
and I can't help crack a big grin
just thinking about the
color and shape of her locket
and what might hide inside.

IVÁN TOO?

After class, my locket's closed
when Magda is around.
I don't bring up my worry about
Mima's crazy moon ceremony idea
which is Teresa's same zany hope for Magda.
The thing is, she doesn't care
despite our Mama Earths.
Magda's flowering hasn't started
I know because she wears undershirts
and not an almost B-size bra like me.

So, I tell her about getting busted.
How I cut up
the picture of my family.
I expect her to laugh
but instead she is kind
as a sleeping kitten
when she defends me,
Sometimes we do things
we don't mean
when we're hurt.

My locket rattles.
I want to talk with Magda about
          things. Important things.

I watch her show me the new trick
she learned on her skateboard
that she watched Iván do from afar.
I figure, my secrets might have
a soft place to land
with Magda.

I undo my locket
and I confess,
          I really like Iván.
Magda stops suddenly and stares
into me like I just slapped her.

          I really like Iván too.

My eyes fill with confusion
How could she?
She's supposed to be
my best friend.

I expected this from Aurora
but from Magda?

I should have never
unlocked
my heart.

SLIPPERY EVERYTHING

Everything I think is

isn't.

Friends that are

aren't.

A boy I like

isn't mine

but everyone's

and

no one's.

A BOY LIKE HIM

She must have seen
my face splatter on the ground.

No, I mean, he's like a boy I want to be.
        Oh, not that you want to be with?
No, nerd, not at all!
If I could, I'd give up being a girl
to be a boy like him right now.
If I could, I'd jump right into his skin.

Really?
I can't imagine it.
I'd have a boy as a best friend?

My thinking face must have bounced up from the floor
and contorted in the air like an acrobat.

Does that freak you out, Celi?

In a split second
I realize no one ever stuck her in a dress

and we never played dolls
or spread pintura on our lips.

We talk about funny things,
outdoor things, bomba drums,
        and we laugh.
A girl not interested
in frilly dresses
nor makeup messes
but warm and kind
and funny and smart.

        Does that freak me out?
        No Magda, it makes you
        as awesome as Iván
        and more.

CONFESSION

Magda is patient with me
as I open my locket just long
enough to unfold this list
of things I love about Iván,

      I love . . .
      The way he never
      fusses with his hair
      the way he talks in a raspy voice
      like he's about to get laryngitis
      and how he smiles with
      only half his mouth
      how he wears his jerseys not too tight
      and corduroys with a slight sag
      nothing that would make Papi frown.
And how he skates!
Magda interrupts.
      Yeah, how he skates like
      he's gliding on the wind.
Yup!
She nods, toothsome and happy.

I close up my locket before
I let her know that
I get a light squirmy feeling
in my chest and sometimes
in my flor
when he
is near.

AURORA'S AURA

I feel a sudden
breeze in the studio.
I look up behind Magda
to see nothing
but the
remnants of a shadow.
A rushed rustling
then someone tripping
and crying, *Ouch!*
Sounds like Aurora's screechy voice
before the sound of shuffling
feet scurries away.

Magda and I look at
each other, begging,
That wasn't Aurora spying?

My head's in a whirlwind.
What if Aurora now also knows
what I hold tight in my locket
with all of my might?

FIRST QUARTER MOON

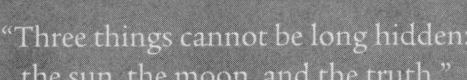

"Three things cannot be long hidden:
the sun, the moon, and the truth."

— *Buddha*

ON OUR DRIVE
TO SCHOOL

The next morning
Juju plays a road game
searches for words
on signs and billboards
in the order of the alphabet.

He spots the *A* in Allah Market
where Mima gets the freshest goat cheese.
Now he's looking for a *B*
and finds it in the last word in
Everett and Jones Barbeque
the place where Papi sneaks off
when veggie Mima's not looking.

He doesn't see what I see.

Our neighbors Mei Lin and Rashad
pressing their three kids
wrapper tight

into a beat-up minivan
like us.

Trucks headed for the hills, carrying
landscaping gear like weapons
to where Papi says only
the loaded rich
get to live
unlike us.

We swivel through the pothole streets.

In the flatlands I can't catch a glimpse
of the Bay's blue still waters
or the bridges that swoon
so far away.

We swerve by the double strollers
        filled with babies
the wire shopping carts
        filled with botes for recycling
the man who wears a tailored African-print suit
        headphones in, at the bus stop
and the woman who has made her tent house
        by the freeway entrance
like so many.

The every color gente
who push those babies to preschool
and dig through the recycling bins
and get to work
and make a home
like us.

They don't make it to Juju's alpha list.

Maybe it's only my locket that loves
the yummy
            crummy
                    lop
            sided
way
East Oakland rolls.

AT AMANECER COMMUNITY SCHOOL

Juju scrambles out of the car
to the lower-grade playground
like a dog on the loose.

I take my time
        strut behind him.
The quick kiss Papi blasted on me
still on my forehead.

I watch him run
make sure he gets
where he needs to safely
because in this K–8 school
you can't always trust
the salty middle schoolers
like me.

WAVES

At the upper-grade quad
I see Aurora from far away
imagine squishing her
scrawny
auburn-
haired
head
like an ant
between my fingers.

I'm secretly grateful that Iván
goes to Orozco Bilingual Academy
nowhere near us.

Then suddenly, I hear a low grumble.
Ms. Celestina Rivera.
When I turn to the teacher calling me
I see it's Magda
practicing her big-dude voice.

We snort laugh 'cause she's fooled me again.

Hey, Celi, so I got this idea. . . .
My eyes wander back to that stinker Aurora
while I listen because I can't help
imagine what she knows.
For our science fair project
I was thinking that maybe
we could do ours about waves.
      What?
My eyes dart back to Magda
      Yeah, waves. That'd be hecka awesome!
And we could make fake waves
in a kiddy pool or something.
      Yeah! Fake waves.

I confess that I wish to make
waves big enough to wipe out
secret-snatching Aurora.

TULIPS IN THE MIRROR

After school
I dread getting in the shower.
I fight with Mima
right before I get in here.
Don't need it.
Don't want to.
Feel too lazy.
But when the warm water

              falls
              on
              my
               body

I escape to the land of lather.
      I never want to leave.

This is where bubbles make my new body
      disappear
and I have my old one back
where I don't have fur-like hair

growing on my legs
or two tulip bulbs on my chest
and my curly hair is not poofy.
It is slick
and long
like a

     s
     i
     r
     e
     n
     a
     's.

Mima has to come into the bathroom
       to get me out.
Be mindful of the drought, mija.
I climb out of the tub and dry myself off.
I catch my reflection in the mirror
and I can't pretend anymore.
   There they are:
       the fuzzy hair, the tulip breasts, my growing thighs.
Mima says I'm flowering early
and it's true, my body is on the way to look like hers
blooming like a flower
I don't want to be.

THE PLAN

I scheme with Magda
about how we are going
to bring Iván closer.

We could invite him to our Farolitos performance in two weeks?
Then we can hang out at the café in the lounge after.
Magda's a genius.

> I already got his number
> from Mima, who has
> a contact list of all the Redwood campers.

> Maybe I can sneak the tablet
> and send him a text?

You gotta be careful not to get caught, Celi.
Magda knows that it could be tricky.

Both of our mothers
are always on health patrol
refuse to get us phones.

Magda's dad *had* to find
an article about it online
that scared them straight
into a crackdown on screens.
They say kids our age
will be affected by the electromagnetic
fields because we are still growing
and really have no business having a phone.

Parents don't always know what's right.
Though they think they do.
Especially herbalist mothers and chiropractor mothers
musician dads and social worker dads
like mine and Magda's
who insist everything is better
when it is grounded to the earth.

In fact, I've known about Iván's number
and dreamt of sending a dozen texts
but never did because I didn't think
I had a reason.

Now that I do, I'm going to wait
until Mima's whipping up some tonic or on the phone
to send him our invitation
in secret.

SMASHED HEART

When I set out to find the tablet
where Mima's been hiding it
Juju's little nose turns up
like he's sniffing something
in the air above him.
Those savage blue eyes
scan my movements
like a wildcat about to pounce on its prey.

I pick up my music book
and begin to practice my vocal scales
purposefully out of tune
and go sit near the window by my bed
which sends Juju running
with his hands over
his sensitive feline ears.

Soon as I see
he's no longer on my trail
I calmly begin
to search the house

quiet, like a thief.

I can hear Mima on the phone
with one of her needy herbal clients
fussing in the kitchen.

Just as I'm about to give up
I find my tablet
tucked inside bedsheets
in the hall closet.

I rush to my bed
I put the tablet
inside my music book
and begin to text.

When I glance up
Juju is standing there
both his fists
on his hips
a big you're-busted smirk
spread across his grill.

When he calls *MIMA!*
I punch him in the chest
as hard as I can.
        Shut up!

He folds over in pain
grabbing his chest
his mouth so open
you can see
his missing baby fangs
but
nothing
is moving in
or out of it.

I shoot to my feet
stand next to him
rub his back briskly
wishing that I had not
punched him in the chest!
      Of all places — did I smash his heart?
I wish that he would
do something
cry
shout
breathe!

     Juju! Juju!

Until finally, he releases
a raspy moan
and I'm so relieved

to hear that cry
that I'm so used to drowning out.
      I'm sorry, Juju!

Words spill from my fear. . . .
      I just didn't want you to tell on me.
      Please don't tell Mima!
      I promise, I'll let you come skateboarding
      with Magda and me.
I plead.

And just like that
he sucks it all back
blinks his tears away
a smile starting to grow
in the corners of his lips.

Really? You promise?

      Yeah, I promise.
      But let me send this text.
      Okay?

Okay, he grins and rubs his chest
like a Cheshire cat who's gotten
away with something so good.

THE INVITATION

      Hey, I wrote.

      It's Celi from camp

Hey is for horses

How'd you get my number?

      Got it from the camp list (toothsome smile emoji)

Oh (brown thumbs-up emoji)

      Wyd?

Homework (poop emoji)

      Lol same

      Wyd in two weeks?

Idk, prolly on my board or at capoeira. Why?

      I was thinking maybe

      you'd like to come see

      my performance

      . . .

      And then hang out at the café at La

      Peña after?

Is it for that bomba

class?

      Yup

I've been watching that

class (peeping eyes emoji)

      Really?

Looks hella chill

Like the drumming the

most tho

      The class ain't nothing

      You should see our shows

      (three fire emojis)

Ooh, scared of you

      So can you come?

Idk, I gotta check w moms

      It's next Sunday 3 - 6

Hold up

. . .

Moms says I'm clear

      Nice (brown thumbs up emoji)

      K gtg

      See u then

Gtg too

Later

(waving hand emoji)

THE TABLET

I hit send in time to hear
Mima's footsteps coming
from the kitchen
where she was also brewing
an aroma of
pozole and love
my favorite stew
that slowly fills the house
with a smell of corn hominy, garlic, and onion
I've known my whole life.

I shove the tablet under my pillow
but Mima sees me yank out
my hand.

Mima barks,
Are you sneaking the tablet again, Celi?
Mija, I have to trust that you are going
to make good choices!
> No I wasn't — my lies choke my last word.
You know you're limited

to using it only once a week.
AND not on a school night
especially when I've taken it from you!

Her temper rises to the stratosphere
when she feels disrespected.
Her alarm for broken rules
turns my warm pozole mama
into a witch as mean as mud.
Especially when I lie some more,
   I'm just checking the weather!

She goes to get the tablet
from under my pillow
but I block her hand
and this makes her frown
in a growing anger.
She fishes furiously and
when she gets it she
scans it to see that
I've actually been texting Iván.

With a quick turn of her body
she ruins me again.
I'll take this. Thank you.

There's no telling when she'll give it back.

MISSION ACCOMPLISHED

At school, when I tell Magda that I got caught
she chuckles but taps my back,
It's okay . . . we knew it was risky.

I quietly beam; I've accomplished my mission.
Mima's been silent about the texts
and hasn't told Papi either.

Did you tell Iván that we would
meet him afterward, to hang out?
              Yup, he'll be expecting to hang out with m—with us.
I turn away so Magda can't see me
bite my lip in a serious uh-oh.
I did not mention Magda at all.

Papi often reminds me to think of others
especially with family, like Juju
but I have a hard time with that one
because I don't want to share

everything with my brother
despite his heart condition
and the trouble I get into over that
somehow makes me wish I didn't
have a little brother at all.

I never meant to not think of Magda.

MIMA'S MOON

Mima cried the news
in her older sister's ear
when she started.

She was scared.
No one had prepared her.
Not her mother, not her sisters.

It came as a stain of blood
so dark she thought
she was sick.

Her sister led her to the bathroom
showed her how to apply a pad
on clean underwear
and said little else.

Mima was ashamed for bleeding
        hid in her bed all night.

She tells me this story over and over

because she doesn't want me
to know her shame
she doesn't want me
to be surprised or have questions.

Though I do, I don't ask her.
Into my locket they go
because my locket doesn't lecture.

She tells me that
our indigenous ancestors
were in tune with natural cycles
held our bleeding to be powerful.
And that during our moon time
women gathered in special huts
to nurture, create, and be in
sacred space with their cycle.
It is my birthright, she insists
to honor my cycle in this same way
so that when my moon comes
I will be ready and proud
to share it with our community.

But I argue,
       I am not purely Mexican
       Papi's dark skin and Caribbean sway
       dance inside me too.

Even though much of our knowledge
was taken away from us
many cultures honored
women's moons across the millennia, Celi.
Both of your lineages grant you that gift.

She points to the sky,
The moon belongs to all women, hija.

When it comes, I don't
want a hut
or a ceremony.
I will hide it from Mima
for as long as I can.
I hope it never comes
because I don't know
how to hide the moon.

PUERTO RICAN DRUM DANCE

I've been dancing bomba
since I was two
or so I'm told.

Our family went to see
master drummers and dancers
from the island visiting Oakland.

During the batey, the native Taíno word
for gathering in a circle
to openly jam,
I watched with Mima from the sidelines
while Papi was invited to drum.
Ms. Susana saw me holding the
bottom tips of my white ruffled dress
imitating the dancers who went
into the circle, one after the other,
to have a single dancing conversation

with the lead drummer.
Ms. Susana took me by the hand
and led me into the batey
for me to try.

I looked back at Mima, unsure,
but her big eyes urged me.

Once inside, I did not copy
what Ms. Susana asked me to
as she danced next to me.
I held the tips of my little dress
and pretended I was catching
butterflies in the air.
That is what the music told me to do
and the lead drummer responded to me
like a reflection in a mirror.
My tiny-footed sandals made
a slight shuffle on the ground
my brow crinkled
my arms and skirt spoke
my first piquetes ever.
It was only for a minute at most
but the entire batey
clapped with joy
as I thanked the lead

drummer with a nod
and left the circle
initiated
and in love.

WHAT PULLS US

It turns out that what
moves a wave is the
moon.

Madga and I find out about that
while sifting through library books
and putting together our wave display board
on my living room floor.
I could have told you that!
fact-crazed Juju interrupts,
The gravitational pull of the moon's orbit
moves all bodies of water on our planet.
Magda throws a piece of crumpled paper at him.
Okay, Señor Cerebro, she teases.
He flinches but then
storms off yelling,
Fine! I'm just saying!

> This is exciting, Magda!
> Our project is going to be the best
> now that we've got Luna involved.

It'll be better than Aurora's boring
presentation on black holes.
Yup! Maybe we can make a papier-mâché moon
put it on a stand somehow.
Maybe build a lever that'll
make the kiddy pool move?

While Magda conjures details
my locket spins.

Am I made of water waves
      that twirl
      and
            crash
    and
              foam?
Is it Luna that
    pulls me
        to
        keep secrets
        to
        heart Iván
        to
        scowl at Aurora
        to
        groove with Magda
        to
        dance?

AT AMANECER COMMUNITY SCHOOL SCIENCE FAIR

The kids swarm like wasps
around each of their projects.
Magda and I know that ours
    is going to rock!
Maybe come in first place?
Her clever lever idea works
like a mechanical charm
and my papier-mâché moon
glows with iridescent paint
    the prettiest Luna you ever saw.
Our fact board was checked and approved
by Teresa and Señor Cerebro himself.
Curious to see our friends' work
Magda and I take a walk and visit
    - a tightrope project about balance

- the five-pound vat of homemade slime
  - Juju's paper airplane launchers that had
        all the elementary kids going wild
but still, we think we're golden
and then
we get to Aurora's.

Wow! says Magda with an extra long *o*
when she sees the biggest display
in the multipurpose room.

A dome covered with black curtains
welcomes you with a red sign that reads:
"Black Hole Ahead — Enter at Your Own Risk."
Magda rushes to get in line to enter
        and drags me with her.
I only wait in line because
I want to see firsthand
        Aurora's flaming fail.

Inside, a gazillion neon drawn-on stars
and glowing ping-pong balls float above us.
Everything is lit by black light
as if we are in space.
At the far end of the dome
a luminescent ring outlines
a big dark cave.

From a speaker, a dull white noise
beeps with random spaceship sounds.
Then Aurora's screechy voice comes on:
A black hole is formed with the death
of a massive star. The collapse creates
a point in space so dense
it begins to suck things into it
by gravity.
If something falls into one
it cannot get out.
Even light can't escape
its gigantic pull!

And BOOM!
A switch is turned on
that sounds like a vacuum.
We watch
as
ping-pong ball
after
ping-pong ball
gets
sucked into
the great
black hole.

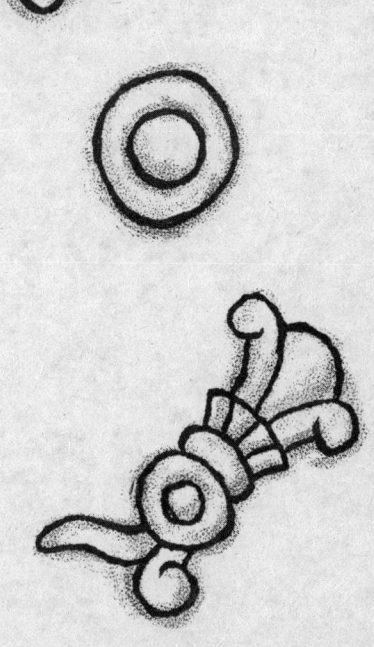

It's brilliant and
I. Can't. Stand it. ➔ *Thats what the girl said in the play!*

I push my way through a crowd of kids.
      Magda swings the curtains open
behind me shaking her head
      and smiling brightly
'cause we just got
      burned
by Aurora.

A BLACK HOLE

At the end of the science fair
Aurora semiskips over to us
petting her
     first-place ribbon
     in her hand
     like a rat.   *Similie*
From her smirk fall
     her condolences.

       Sorry that your wimpy moon waves
       didn't move the judges.
       And too bad that Iván wasn't here
       to see my winning display.

Congrats! Magda taps Aurora on the shoulder.
Your black hole project was hecka amazing.
At the same time
she holds me by the arm.
     She knows
       I want to charge.
I bite my nails to stop me from speaking.
I grin growl behind my fingers
     and wish that Aurora

would
fall
into
a black hole
to
never
escape.

I've been that before!

MORE THAN EVER

For the next week
Magda and I up our
game for the performance
like two athletes training for a win.
Iván's coming to see us!

We beg Ms. Susana to let us be
lead dancer and drummer for a seis corrido.
It's the fastest bomba rhythm
and the one that lets me
dance without a skirt
move my shoulders and hips the most
unlike the other rhythms that rely on
skirt technique and shoulders mostly.

In a seis corrido
Magda's echo is precise
she doesn't delay
to beat the drum at every
shake and strut of my hips
or in the up-and-down bounce

of my shoulders
making our communication
shine above the other drummers,
stick players, maraca players, and singers
in what Papi calls
beautiful Afro-Puerto Rican syncopation.

Iván's not going to know what hit him.

SHOWTIME

La Peña is packed!
Backstage, my head is wrapped tight in a headscarf and bun
a big turquoise flower pinned to the left side of my headwrap
to match my turquoise flowered ankle-length skirt
that makes me feel like the ocean.
I put a dash of lip gloss on my lips
so they shimmer beneath the lights.
Magda wears her deep blue guayabera,
white jeans, sneakers, and a hat
she borrowed from her dad.
She tugs the Kangol down low
an anchor on the short crop of her hair.
We stand side by side in the big mirror
Are you ready? she asks my reflection.
I move to high-five her reflection
then stop and turn to high-five the real her.
We both giggle as we clasp hands
snap our fingers and flutter them away like birds.

I look for Iván in the audience

before the MC announces the show.
I don't see his bright eyes and bushy eyebrows
        anywhere.
Still, Magda and I lock in
when our seis corrido is called.
        We enter the world of drums,
song, and movement we all create
and we're on point
just like we rehearsed.

I am no longer Celi who bites
her nails, has secrets to spare,
and got blown away by Aurora.
I am Celi waxing
                circling
                        shaking my body
            making rhythms of my own
                a release of my heart
                    my joy.
Papi would say the ancestors are with me.
I don't doubt him because I feel their pride
as I glide and turn and burn on the stage.

The audience of our parents and friends
roars in hoots and hollers when we are done!
We can't see them, the bright stage lights blind us

but I know that Magda, like me
wishes that Iván is in the audience too
there to witness the best we've ever done.

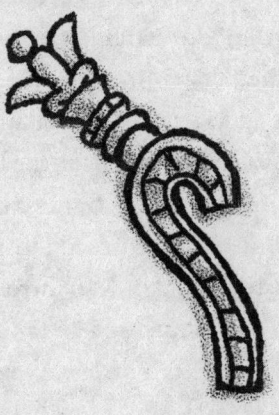

LA PEÑA CAFÉ

When the houselights come up
we see Iván standing there with two other boys
who look a klutzy twelve like him.
He brought a crew!
He sees me and signals to the café.
I shoot him a thumbs-up and move
to collect my things.

We make our way over to the restaurant
to find that he and his friends
are sitting around a couch and coffee table
their skateboards propped against the wall.
All of our parents are milling about ordering wine, talking
and I ask Mima for an agua fresca — guayaba, my favorite —
and Magda asks her dad, Luis, for the same, her favorite too.
We come to sit near the boys and I swallow hard
and suddenly I want to bite off a hangnail on my thumb.
But I don't, instead I introduce Magda to Iván
which stirs him to introduce his friends to us.
This is Pedro and Leandro.
Iván looks a little nervous.

His eyes shift from mine to Magda's.
What kind of dude name is Magda? he blurts.
It's short for Magdalena I defend.
Magda holds my shoulder so she can speak.
Everyone's always called me Magda
and the dude clothes is just who I am.

So you're a girl? You look straight-up like a boy!
Iván covers his laugh with his fist
and turns to his friends
who are chuckling with disbelief.

Like I said, I dress like who I am.

Iván snorts and continues to snicker.
Oh snap, I thought only men could drum in bomba!
Well at least that's what Aurora told me.
That you're just faking it.

Magda takes a deep breath
the hurt only showing itself in
her trembling lower lip.

FYI, women drum all the time in bomba.
Besides, what does it matter, Iván? I get loud at him.
Can we sit or what?

I don't know, we don't usually hang with freakazoids.
I don't care how much you like my skateboarding.

The dizzying feeling for him
that was swooshing inside moments before
     sizzles in anger now, and for Aurora too.
Now I *know* she shared our secrets.
I shove him hard on his chest,
tug my friend by the hand and say,
     C'mon Magda, who needs these jerks.

CRACKED

Magda and I find shelter backstage
now clear of all performers
both of our hearts
cracked and beginning to ooze.

I feel I need to make excuses.
   Blame Aurora, the twerp.
   He's never acted that way before.
   So cruel. So rude.
I thought he knew I was hanging out too?
I confess, I didn't think to mention her.
Magda frowns into a sadness
I had never seen before
and comes with tears
that fall
   on her cheeks
   like slow
   drops
   of rain.

I'm sorry, Magda, for not thinking of you.
I'm so sorry, Magda, for what he said.

He's not the boy we thought he was.

TEA AND TABLET

At home, Mima gives back the tablet
as reward for the performance.
Also gives me honey manzanilla tea.
She can see I am quiet
but doesn't ask why.

I don't want to touch the tablet
because I'd have to see his last text
before I knew the kind of fool
he really is or that I am.

Juju is playing with his Legos
and talking like he does
about who messed up
during the show and why.

I look out my window for Luna.
Where is she tonight?

She is nowhere.
She is in her dark phase

our time for potential Mima says
the time to plant seeds
that will bloom when the moon is full.

I think about Iván, Aurora, Magda, and my foolishness.

What will we harvest when the seeds planted are so mean?

THE INVITATION REVERSED

The following Friday night
I'm on the tablet watching a movie
when a text comes through.
Sup my Celi?
It's from Iván.
I begin to answer,
      Leave me alone, I don't text with jerks!
but I pause before I send it
because he is typing too.
My curiosity grows bigger than my anger.

. . .

It's my birthday
tomorrow
Going with some of the
guys to the movies
You wanna come?

I hit send.

What?
So does this mean no?
      Yes
Yes you'll come or yes it
means no? (crazy face pleading emoji)
I'm only inviting a few
guys, c'mon it'll be hella fun
Then that familiar flutter in my panza returns
and I feel an   ebb back to him.
      What are you watching?
 Jurassic Attack (three dinosaur emojis)
      Will your mom be there?
Nah it's a drop-off
I'm turning 13 (emoji smile with glasses and
bucked teeth)
      My mom probably won't
      let me.
LMK
show starts at five
Grand Lake Theatre.
      K

My locket is in a tussle
      tattered battered
      but lifted.

I hear Magda's words,

  Sometimes we say things we don't mean when we are hurt.

Maybe, I just don't know what's hurt Iván

for him to have said the things he did to Magda.

My curious locket wants to know and so

I ask permission.

Mima says I can go

but

only if she and Juju

can find another movie to watch

at the same time in an adjacent theater.

The flesh-eating dinosaurs would frighten Juju.

Lucky for me, a penguin movie is playing

and I can go and be one of the guys

with Iván, Pedro, and Leandro

but not really.

NOT SO SECRET

I know I will never be able to tell Magda.
But it is something my locket cannot hide.
Mima, Juju, Pedro, and Leandro know too.
My mind is mush.
Right now
I can't think about
how to keep this secret safe.

Tomorrow, I'm going to the movies with Iván!

THE MOVIES

In the lobby, I buy Iván popcorn
and hand him a medicine satchel
I threw together for him
for skateboarding first aid:
      tea tree oil to disinfect
      tepezcohuite salve to heal a scrape
      bandages, medical tape, gauze.
He thanks me with a slight shove on one shoulder.

Iván saves a seat for me next to him
so we can share the popcorn.
I can't think of anyone but Magda at first
and how she might want to be here too
but I'm distracted by Mima and Juju
who've come all the way up to our seats
just to see where I'm at!
I clench my jaw at her and shoo her away
then the movie starts.
            I forget Magda and Mima
                 get lost in the terror on-screen.
I'm eating popcorn instead of my nails

and so is Iván.
I reach into the bucket of popcorn
he reaches in after me
grabs my buttery hand and
                        holds it there
lost in the movie too.
I look at him
                slip out my hand
from under his
        my flor more sparkly than ever.
I pick up my root beer with two hands
sip in the flavor of this
                excitement and fear.
Not so much because of the movie
anymore but because now I know
what it's like
                to have held a boy's hand.

He leans in and whispers, *Are you scared?*
        A little, I confide.
Though he's asking about the movie.
For a moment, I wish to be in the theater next door
watching the penguin film
with Mima and Juju.
That thought is cast aside
        by a buttered locket
                a held locket

beaming to be here
      without Mima and Juju.

I flow open.
Swim in all of the special attention
he's giving me.
I am warm and feel like
     i'm floating
when he simply turns to me to ask,
Can I have a sip of your root beer?

WHEN I TURN THIRTEEN

When do you turn twelve? One thick eyebrow rises.
            Soon, I'm a summer baby.
    Would your parents let you have a . . .
Oh, never mind, he sighs.

Inside thoughts tumble like weeds.

                          What
            would   it
    be   like
    to   be
            his   girl
                    friend?
Have a first kiss
        on the lips.
                His
really touching mine.
My parents would never allow it.
Papi says, I have to be thirty
and Mima says I have to be thirteen

when I'll also be able to wear makeup
and crop tops, have a phone,
and go to the mall without a chaperone.
Why do I have to wait for all of the
good things when I don't feel
like a baby anymore?

But maybe Iván only likes
to have me around
to be one of the guys
and was just gonna ask
about something else.

SECRETS IN THE DARK

Our movie lets out.
Mima and Juju are still in there
so we wait by the large cardboard dinosaur display.
When they come out of their movie
Iván thanks Mima for letting me come
and asks how the movie was for them.
Mima loves it when kids look
an adult in the eye when talking.
Juju erupts in mental diarrhea,
                So, Celi, how was your date?
I fume and instantly throw a Junior Mint at him
then cover his mouth with my hand.
Juju pries away my fingers and spills,
You haven't even had your moon ceremony
but Mima let you go in there by yourself anyway.
Mima gathers Juju to her while fake smiling
to stop me from attacking him.
Then Iván asks,
What's a moon ceremony?

I feel like someone is stepping
on my chest
my breath stolen away.

It's a beautiful coming-of-age ritual
that our indigenous ancestors
held for young girls before quinceañeras.
Mima is now oversharing with IVÁN!
I don't know what to do with myself so I try to tug Juju's ears
but Mima pulls him behind her and farther away from me.
Cool, like something the Aztecs did? Iván nods and
looks at me sort of cross-eyed
but then winks.

Iván refuses a ride home
prefers to skate with the boys.
As we leave, we watch them ride off
on their boards though it is getting dark.
Just enough night to see that Luna
watches over them too.

I don't tell Mima about
his holding my hand inside the movies
the almost girlfriend question
or what he thinks about Magda.

These nuggets are for my locket to keep.

COME OVER

Sunday morning I awake
to Juju talking to himself
about being cold in early June,
You know that water freezes
at thirty-two degrees Fahrenheit?
Since we are made of water
we can freeze too.

The almost-summer mornings
in Oakland wouldn't be
so cool if it weren't
for the fog that rolls across
the Bay like a wet blanket
and seeps into these old walls
with no insulation
the crisp wood floors
of our little house
that seems to be more
alive because of the bold
teals, reds, mustard yellows

that punctuate the walls
in each of the different rooms.

My eyes still closed
I hear the whispers of the freeway
relive every moment from the day before
a silent choreography in my mind.

I get a text
from Teresa's phone number, from Magda.
Need to talk to you
In person
Can you come over?
         Today?
Ya
Anytime

Too stunned to say no.
She'll see right through me.
Maybe she already knows
and that's why she needs to talk to me?

Guilt rides on me
like a backpack too full of books.

As I get ready to go see her
Mima says that the rest of the family

has been invited too.
But Papi's got a gig
and Juju is his roadie today.
Anyway, I can't imagine Magda sharing
anything too personal with them.

NOT MAGDA

Magda stands at the door, next to Luis.
Her always smile eclipsed by an almost frown.
They ask us to remove our shoes.

I feel as transparent as a screen.

We don't go into her room
to hang out like we normally do.
We are invited to sit on cushions in a small circle
on the living room floor with our mothers and her dad.
A clay bowl of dried white sage branches
sits at the center.

Teresa ignites the sage, lets it
come aflame, and then blows it out.
She douses her limbs, her head, her chest
with the swirling bitter-smelling smoke.
Luis, Mima, and Magda do the same.
When I am handed the smoking branch
my eyes water, it trembles in my hand.

	The smoke will reveal everything.
Still, I smudge my body
keep the sage near my chest
gather the smoke in the
cup of my hand
pull it into
my heart, my heart, my heart.

When Teresa speaks finally
the words that come out of her
are foreign. . . .
Our child has arrived at a new truth.
A real self, an authentic self, the reality always meant to be.
Marco is his true name.
Magda is part of his historia, the earlier chapters of girlhood.
Also born a boy energy into the body of a girl
it is the wisdom of the sacred masculine placed
in the body of the divine feminine.
We could not claim it for him
until he was ready to understand on his own.
In our ancestral Mexica tradition, Ometeotl
is our Creator spirit that is neither
female nor male but both — divine duality.
Marco has Ometeotl energy
a person who inhabits two beings
the female and the male at once.
Though we can't be certain how our

ancestors felt about people of two energies
because there is so much we don't know
so much we are still learning
as new Mexica, we regard it an honor
to be a reflection of the Creator.

I look over at Magda and fight confusion
a boy in the body of a girl?
I have always known that she was different
a tomboy for sure, more free than anything else
but simply Magda, Magdalena Teresa Sánchez.
Not Marco Sánchez!
Not Marco Magdalena Teresa Sánchez!

Mima taps me back to attention
when Luis begins to speak.
From what we do know
people who danced between
or to other energies
than what they were assigned at birth
were sometimes called xochihuah.
Xochitl is the word for flower in Nahuatl
and a xochihuah is
        the one who bears flowers.
They were known to worship
at the temple of Xochipilli, the flower prince god
who protected people of all gender identities

and queer folks.
Marco, my son, carries the blossoms
of his truth inside him
as a sacred xochihuah.

A sho-chee-wah? I stretch to pronounce
unable to hide
           my unraveling thoughts.
Yes, a xochihuah,
my truth
Magda assures.

I look up to the light
of hopeful
you-understand-me eyes
and all of a sudden
I do somehow
and it's easy.
I pause only to find
my own it's-all-right look
to offer.

I see Magda's hands shake a little
when she says,
Being Marco feels good
even if I have two energies.
My parents say that I don't have to decide yet.

That's part of my road to figuring it all out.
But I feel more boy than girl at the moment.
And because I can be both
I'm going with Marco for right now.

Then Teresa turns to me,
We need your help to make his transition
as a xochihuah safe and loving within the community.
And though we don't know
how we will reveal it
there will be those who will judge.
We need everyone's support and no
one more than yours, Celi.

I feel the weight of Teresa's words
fall feather light on my shoulders
wound up in the love I have for my best echo.

I nod my head slowly.

Magda smiles. No. Marco smiles.
Reaches to squeeze my hand.
The wide white doves of his teeth
are proof of his faith in me.
He is grateful I have his back.

AMIFRIEND DEL ALMA

Marco and I reason
in Spanish, the word *friend* has a gender:
amigo, male
amiga, female
as do many other words.
Friend in English has none.
But in Spanglish, our happy mixed-up tongue,
amifriend has both
the warm sound of *amor* in *am*
and *friend*, the sweetest word English can muster.

NO BAD WITHOUT GOOD

Marco is optimistic,
I hope that others will get me like you, Celi.

But then again, there will be the Ivá ns
who will mock and sneer and hurt
and never understand him
ignorant of Ometeotl and xochihuah, blind to the honor.

No hay mal que por bien no venga.
Marco's right, there isn't anything bad
that does not bring something good.
If it hadn't been for Iván and his friends
Marco thinks he would have never changed a thing.
Celi, it was right then and there that I finally got it!
I knew that I couldn't pretend anymore.

      But maybe you would have without them?
Maybe. Well, at least we don't have to deal with Iván ever again.

Our clasp, snap, bird-flight-fingers handshake
seals our understanding.
Inside, I wince.

FULL MOON

ECHO MOVEMENT

Marco asks Ms. Susana
and most his teachers, including Papi,
to simply call him Mar instead of Magda.
Mar is the word for *sea* in Spanish.
He wasn't ready to go all the way there
with every one of the kids in bomba class
or in world drums class or at school.
Though most of us could sense
his new kind of happiness.
His parents said they would do that carefully, perhaps
with a community gathering, or a letter
so it is the safest for him.

When we echo, it does not matter
where our gender lands
what our lockets hold
we are body movement
drum movement
song movement
creativity in movement.

Ten minutes before class ends
Iván walks in holding his skateboard.
My heart crinkles and shakes outside of me.
He watches the class like a begging puppy
I think he wants to join
and I feel sorry for him.

MORE THAN THE OTHER

When class is over, Marco
helps put away the drums.
I shove my skirt into my bag
and then I feel Iván standing behind me,
Did you get my texts? He sounds anxious.
I've texted you about a hundred times.
You mad at me or something?
I signal him to follow me as I walk
toward the café away from Marco.
He continues,
Or did your mom take away your tablet again?
I want to tell him that it was a mistake
to have gone to the movies with him
that I really can't be friends with a person
who totally misunderstood and hurt my best friend
no matter how my heart spins.
But I don't.
It is as if my mouth shrinks with the truth.

I'm sorry, yeah, mom's got my tablet.
Whew! I was hecka worried for a minute.
You know, Pedro said that he had a nightmare
after the movie. Can you believe it? A nightmare!
Iván waves his arms and imitates a screaming Pedro.
I giggle to imagine Pedro thrashing in his bed
because he's got to be almost six feet though thin as a pin
but then my laughing grows partly because
my stomach is a ball of nerves.
I double over
suspended in breath
in that   quiet
right before I

                    explode

with laughter.

Celi, what's going on?
Why are you laughing with this creep?
I am disarmed, my laughing slows
but the happy orange warmth
for Iván doesn't leave my chest.
Iván turns to Marco and flails
his arms at him too.

        Come on Mar, see, he's harmless.
I hope Marco will get his humor.
Hey, Magda, can your hair get any butchier?
Iván flings the question at Marco

looking for another laugh.

I'm Mar, not Magda, you idiot!

And I can't be a butch when I'm . . .

He pauses as if wasting his breath,

Can you be any stupider, Iván? Marco finishes.

He's Mar now, Iván, I manage to inject.

Iván bursts out laughing.

You're the funniest-looking Mar I've ever seen!

Marco turns to me, his eyes tearing to shreds.

You call this harmless, Celi?

How could you defend such a jerk?

Before I can really remember my promise

to help Marco I sass,

Oh c'mon, Marco, give him a break

not everyone is going to understand

your changes from one day to the next.

Not everyone's got moms in a women's circle like us.

Marco steps back in disbelief.

A shadowlike hurt travels across his face

when he storms,

Celi! He knows about everything now

because of your big mouth!

I know he did not recognize me.

I did not recognize myself.

Marco is my amifriend

but right now I want

Iván to like me   more.

Want to be invited
to the movies again
for him to hold my hand again
maybe learn to do
fancy skateboard tricks
and go to the
skate park
with him too.

BETRAYING SEA

My locket lies open on
    a shore of a sea
        of confusion
steady sand grounds my feet
like Marco—best amifriend forever
    but the waves of Iván
        crash into me
    a foam that wraps around my legs
        sends a tingle through my body
          and swarms my heart
        with a feeling of
first love?
        His tide draws me
          wants me
            to swim
          in the thrill
       of those waters
            no matter if he's been mean
            once or twice
            and I could drown.

Though I hear Marco's voice calling my name
                      waves feel stronger than sand.

   Maybe with time, he will
        learn to be cool with Marco.
          I reason.
          I hope.

THE LAST DAYS
OF SCHOOL

The next time I see Marco
at school, he looks the other way
hides the bright teeth that spread joy.
Passes by me in the hall as if I don't exist
and the next time
and the next.
I can't blame him.

So I shoo away the emptiness I feel
by pretending to be writing
in my notebook but really playing
MASH a million times.
I rig it by writing:

       Iván

       Iván

       Iván

       Iván

in all four slots of possible husbands.
This way, I will marry Iván no matter

if I drive a beat-up car
have ten children
live in a shack.

I avoid Aurora's suspicious beetle eyes
for just a few more days before summer break.
      Instead, I wonder
what Iván is eating for lunch and
who he is talking to at this very moment.
Will there be a text from him
      waiting
for me when I get home?

WORLD DRUMS CLASS

I sit next to Marco during class
so that Papi doesn't suspect
that Marco's not speaking to me.
      I don't try to look for his eyes.
Marco shuffles his body to
the opposite side of the chair
inch by inch, away from me.
Don't think he wants Papi
to know either
      but I can't be sure.

Papi always sprinkles his lessons
with drum wisdom nobody asks for,
The African tradition of the drum
helps heal mental illness, problems of any kind
the layered rhythms they provide
soothe the brain with left and right brain communication
and ignite the body to stir out of its rut
from any place it might be stuck.

Maybe it was the drum that helped Marco
find his way to himself and not Iván at all.

Marco stays after class to speak to Papi
though his own dad is waiting in the car.
I hang out in the far corner watching
I don't hear them but I wonder
if Marco is telling on me
or if Papi is teaching Marco
how to sing from within
how to tune
the drum inside himself.

PARTNERS

When Marco leaves, I help Papi and Juju
put away the remaining drums.
My eyes squint while I wait for a scolding
but instead he says,
Marco lleva la música por dentro.
She, I mean, HE carries the music deep inside
like Juju and you, Celi.
My eyes pop open while I point to my chest — me?
Except your body is your instrument.
That's why you two make such great partners.
I almost smile and shake my head
hoping the guilt I feel will scoot off
like a nagging bug, but it doesn't.
You can't have dance without music.
Papi keeps talking . . .
but I don't register any more words.
Betraying Marco feels like
a huge bug has landed on my head
and its shameful venom drips down
like egg on my face.

SOLSTICE LOCUST LAKE

Summer solstice swept away
the last days
of school like a swift broom.

Marco is nowhere.

My parents force me to come
to a community solstice celebration
at Lake Merritt where
large layers of smooth grass extend
out from the gray-green water.
All of Oakland's colors
are a rainbow
      splashed and
            spread across the park.
  Salseros dance a rueda on the concrete flat near the arches.
  A hip-hop cypher's going off near the barbecue pits
  and there's a capoeira roda over near the playground.

Others picnic or
run
      walk
          skate
             ride
                 around the paths
while the 580 freeway roars
like a swarm of locusts above our heads.

Then there's my family who
sets up our batey
in a sunny grassy field
littered with geese poop.

TRÁGAME TIERRA

Now that I'm here, I feel
the warm sun
soothe my grump.
But then I see
Aurora's family, the Camachos
begin to load in.
I wish it were Marco's family
arriving.

      Mima, can you text Teresa?
      Ask if they are coming?
Okay, mija, let me see.
She fumbles with her phone.

I help Mima lay out
our gray-and-white-striped Mexican blanket
and put out the food:
      nopal salad and tostadas
      black beans and rice
      and Papi's garlic chicken.

I check her phone for an answer.
Nothing.

Papi's tuning the drums
and Juju hit the playground
the moment we got here.

I follow Mima's eyes
searching for Juju
and then I spot him!

Iván, near the playground
standing over a woman
with long black locks
spiraled into a ponytail
reading a book
not too far from the capoeira roda.

Isn't that your friend Iván? Mima asks.
      Um, yeah.
*Looks like that might be his mom. I'm
going to say hi.* Mima rises.
You coming, Celi?
      No!
It's a good thing I'm sitting
because I fall back into the blanket
and cover my eyes with my hands.

Okay, suit yourself.

I peek through my fingers and watch
Iván greet Mima with his wonky smile
and introduce her to the woman, who really
does look like she could be his mom.
Mima sits on their blanket
and points over at me!

Iván begins to walk over.

I wish Mama Earth would swallow me whole
but all I can do is press my fingers tighter to my eyes
pretend to be asleep
and pray that Mama Earth is hungry.

ON THE BLANKET

Too much light for you, Celi? Iván squawks.

He plops down next to me.
      I peel myself up from the blanket.
          Force a hi.

Iván's curls sway in the breeze
behind him, the lake's water reflects the solstice sun
makes it look like he's got an aura of lava around him.

His voice breaks again.
So when's your dad gonna play?
      I dunno, it's a free-for-all.
I'm really beginning to like bomba.
      I can tell.
Really? You've seen me hella stalk your class, eh?
I shrug and answer,
      You don't have to be Puerto Rican to play bomba
      you know.
No?
Marco's Mexican and he plays, I want to say

but instead I say,
> Well, no. You aren't Brazilian
> and you play capoeira. Right?
> It's a feeling, and you know
> if it's got you and you've got it.

Before we know it
our moms are laughing
and eating together
and the bomba drums
and the cantos
are fired up.

Iván's capoeira master, Mestre Tamborim,
whistles Iván over for his turn to play in the roda.

I exhale   for the first time
since he sat there
but then I hold my breath
> again
when he says,
Be right back.

SICK

I dig through Mima's purse
for her phone.

Now I hope Marco's *not* coming!

Teresa answered:

> *Sorry amiga, Marco's*
> *not feeling well.*
> *Let's connect in a couple*
> *of weeks when you and the*
> *kids get back from LA. Okay?*

A tornado of relief and worry unleashes inside me.
It'll be another two weeks without Marco
and a trip to LA I didn't even know about!
And Marco's not feeling well?
I've got to tell Mima
maybe one of her herbal concoctions
will make him better.
But what if it's me?
Maybe Marco's
sick   of   me.

INSIDE CIRCLES

I see Aurora go over
to the capoeira circle
to watch Iván, of course
to see him clap his hands
to the music
and wait for his turn
to battle-dance
in the roda.

I turn away thinking
Iván didn't sit next to *her* and she knows it.

I look over at Papi playing the lead drum, the primo.
He points his lips at the center of our batey.
Though I hesitate to grab my skirt because
there is no one like my echo
I remember what Papi told us
about our black Puerto Rican
ancestors who created bomba.

They would dance and drum
after a long day's work
as slaves on the plantations
to erase their pains.
It is how they kept their spirits alive.
If they lifted their skirts when
they were tired and hurt
I have no room to complain.

Then, I think about all the circles
I see and know:
       the Puerto Rican batey
       the salsa rueda
       the capoeira roda
       the Mexica círculo
       the drum
       this lake
       the sun
the moon.

I've got to get up and get into the circle
for a solstice bomba dance for all of us.

RHYTHM

Iván comes back
in time to see
me hit my last piquete
and Papi's last drum response.

When I come out of the batey
Iván's sitting with Mima
AND Aurora on our blanket!
      Every one of my nerve endings cringes.
Too late to turn around because
my feet are already walking that way.
My fingers go straight to my chewing teeth
and when I arrive Mima scorns,
Celi, las manos.
You killed it, Celi, Iván beams right into me.
Mima shines, *I could watch her dance forever.*
Before I can say thank you
Aurora snaps,
You were off time, you know.
      I was suspending time, genius.
      You'd know that if you

knew about rhythm.
Iván snickers through his nose
in the cutest way.
Celi, be nice, Mima's voice is seriously low.
Aurora shrugs,
I do know about rhythm
because I'm full Puerto Rican
not like some people.
She clears her throat
and rolls her eyes sideways.

      If Mima weren't here I'd be
            tackling Aurora to the ground
       and pushing her into the
          stripes of the blanket.

Mima reaches over and gently swats my
hand out of my mouth, knows
that maybe I'm thinking
something devious.

What you doing next week, Celi?
Iván asks suddenly.
You wanna go to the skate park?
Aurora jumps in, *sounds fun, which one*
are we going to?
I glare at her.

Iván crinkles his face
in an are-you-crazy kind of way.
I was asking Celi!
I can't help but beam
a big fat so-silly grin
to see Aurora's
shoulders
shrink
into a frown.

When I answer,
        That'll be cool.
I don't tell either of them that
next week, I'll probably be in LA
missing the skate park
with Iván.

OAKLAND TO EL-A

Yeya, my six aunts
and my cousins in Los Angeles
are a woven rug
of laughter and bickering
that always welcomes us
with the Mexican warmth
of LA's desert heat.

Though Papi stays behind
this time
because of a gig
and my locket is more
achy than ever without Marco
LA feels like home too.

    El-A is:

    Yeya and her cazuelas
    filled with beans and amor.

    Tias who wear

too-tight clothes and
manicured nails
to work at dentist offices
and in computer programming
and in real estate
and to stay at home with their kids . . .

Cousins too young to hang out
with me but who are the perfect
half dozen to
dog pile on Juju
during water balloon fights.

XOCHIHUAH IN CONCRETE

I escape to Yeya's brick patio
to the hammock beneath the avocado tree.
Though it is daytime, I see a faint sliver of Luna
peeking through the big leaves.

I sneak the tablet and text Marco
but he doesn't answer.
He seems as far away as Luna.
I ignore Iván's text about the skate park.
I don't care that Iván's tide is waning.

    While I rock

                    back and forth
      forth and back
I notice how all of Yeya's
plantas — the sábila

           the yerba santa

              the hydrangeas
           the roses

                    the jacalosúchil
          have found a way to grow
no matter the cold cement
that surrounds them.

Like Marco
a xochihuah
who's put up
with the awful
concrete of me.

HAMMOCK LIMPIA

As if she can read minds
Yeya asks me about Marco
when she finds me on the
hammock.

I play it off
      I dunno, Yeya, I haven't seen him for weeks.
Yeya's soft round hands
stroke my hair as she showers
me with sweet Spanish
words that never feel heavy like Mima's.

You have to be strong for him, Celi.
He doesn't have an easy road.

I only nod my betraying head
too ashamed to speak.

My comadre, Chuyina, had a similar but different experience.
Her family in Mexico never understood
her ways, that she would leave being a man

to be herself, a woman.
Her father threw her out of the house.
So she had to come pa'l Norte
where she thought no one would judge her
but sometimes they still do.

   That's so sad, Yeya. You wouldn't know
   she's been through so much
   because she's always smiling.
Si, well, whenever Chuyina feels like it's too much
she comes to me for a limpia.

All I do is take this
Palo Santo and light it
and I fan the smoke onto her body
so that it floats away her worries.
It makes her feel lighter
every time she is hurt.
Here. I want you to
take some to offer Marco.

She puts two thick
sweet-smelling sticks
in my hand and wraps
my fingers around them
and blows into my fist.

She looks at me with pride
her two
long gray braids
sway like this hammock
behind her back
as she walks away.

If Yeya knew what
was hurting Marco
right now
she'd give
me
a limpia.

THE SILENT DRUM

With each passing day
my locket feels weighted.
It still has no echo.

Finally, back in bomba class
I listen for his drumming
but he refuses to play when I come up.
Each time, he has a bathroom emergency
and lets the other drummers fill in for him
and when Ms. Susana forces him to drum
and I dance, he switches from lead drum
to sticks or maracas.

I no longer want to dance.
He no longer wants to drum.

A silent drum is the sound
my heart makes when it is hurting.
My locket is no use.
His silence crushes me from the inside out.

My locket rebels, I want my echo back!
I'm not sure if I want
Iván   more
anymore.

AMIGA LUNA

I take to staring at the moon
      each night
      when I can find her.

A big glowing circle in the sky
      beautiful
      alone
sometimes a tiny sliver
sometimes strong
filled with pockmarks
      imperfect like me.

I imagine I cling to stars
to get there and sit and ask,
      Luna, what do I do?
      How do I make an
      echo without Marco?
She only answers with
her own loneliness and then
      she fades.

If she is so powerful
she pulls tides
why can't she pull some
sense into me
and make me apologize?

I fear I've gone too far.
Hurt too much.

Luna is there despite
how I have treated Marco.

She is a true friend
unlike me
always there
even when she
is hidden to me
and I am hidden too.

SUMMER

Oakland's summer days come down on us
like sheets of gold so warm
we don't need blankets at night.
The only chill I feel is from Marco's freeze.
Still, he hasn't told on me.
Mima, Papi, Juju, Teresa, and Luis don't say a thing.

The only one to notice is Ms. Susana
who has given up on trying to pair
her two best students.
She doesn't believe in forcing art
and asks me to sing instead.

Aurora's all about it and snickers
when Marco ignores me
so proud that she had a hand in the silence
but maybe more happy that now she gets
to be lead dancer.

I wish her boca would shrivel up
like a chicharrón or that I could

punch her in the chest so hard
it would kick-start her cold heart.
I stop myself because
it wouldn't bring Marco back.

Ms. Susana announces that
we have to come to a three-hour
dress rehearsal on Friday
for La Peña's summer performance.
She raises her voice
over our chatter,
Everyone must wear white pants and a white top.
Girls, please wear your bomba skirts over your pants.

I will have to wear my turquoise skirt
even though I'm not dancing.

MOONSHADOW

At dress rehearsal
while Ms. Susana is caught up
in the office dealing with the show's program
all of the kids play a game of silent freeze tag
so Ms. Susana doesn't yell at us
for being too loud when
she comes back.

Marco doesn't play.
He sits at the drum and waits
for Ms. Susana to return.
But I do.

We are swift white shadows
running and freezing, waiting and tagging
our feet sliding on the slick wood studio floors.

I'm not it and I feel like I have to pee
        but I hold it.
I want to get through this round.
        I dash away, huffing.

Suddenly, I feel Marco
        tug me off to the side
                then drag me backstage.
Still panting from running
my breath escapes between words.
        Now, Marco?
        You wanna talk now?

Celi, your white pants, there is blood all over them.

He points.
Pity and concern
painted across his face.
I look down in shock.

        What?

        The inside of
        my pant legs
        and crotch
        are soaked
        bright
        red.

MOON HAS COME

I am bleeding but it doesn't hurt.
If this is my power, why is it such a mess?
Am I a woman now?
I want to play freeze tag.
I want unstained pants.
I'm not ready.
I burst like
a swollen fruit
and cry.

STAIN

Marco moves quickly.
Here, go into the bathroom stall.
I've got some coins . . . I'll get you a pad.
    Marco, can you also go get my backpack, please?
    I can change into my street clothes.
Hand me your pants and I'll soak them in the sink.
I worry that Ms. Susana will probably
be mad at me for not wearing white pants anymore.
    Please don't tell Ms. Susana that it came
    and that I've made a mess of myself.
Don't worry, I won't tell anyone.

Celi, our moms told us this would happen.
    I know but why now? It's just so embarrassing.
You don't have to tell me about embarrassing.
Imagine what it's going to be like for me to buy pads at the store.
Besides, I don't think anyone saw it but me.
    Thank you, Marco, I whimper.
I want to apologize but my soggy tears
clog my voice and it sounds muddy.
    I'm so sorry, Marco.

Don't cry, Celi. It'll all work out.
His words wash over me as if all is forgiven
even though his forgiveness
is something I haven't earned.

Soon though
I will *have to* tell him the truth
about all I've done — the movies, the texting, the park.
How could I have ever turned my back on him?

A WIDE-OPEN CLASP

There is no more hiding
when Mima sees that I'm
not wearing white pants
like the rest of the kids in class.

I can't hide the big wad
of paper towels wrapped
around my soiled white
pants I carry in my hands.
I'll need them washed
for tomorrow.

Mostly, she sees the currents
of disbelief, fear, and newness
moving across the river of my
reddened face
my defeated face
my uncertain face.

Mima hugs me tightly and kisses me.
Her tenderness and love forces
my locket's clasp wide open
and I don't cry anymore.

The moon is yours now too, mija.

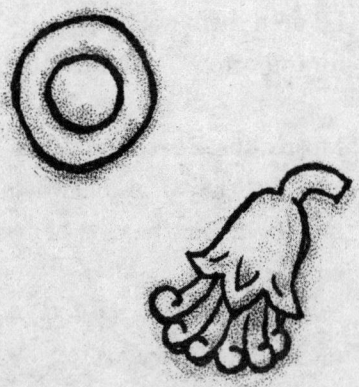

HUMMINGBIRD HERBS

When we get home, Mima runs a hot bath for me.
She gathers fresh herbs from her summer garden
manzanilla, ruda, flores de romero, albahaca
and from her herbal medicine pantry
dried calendula, tila, lavender flowers, and arnica
puts them all in a cheesecloth pouch
in what looks like a giant tea bag
to steep in my bath.

I can hear her hum softly as I slide into the water.
These herbs will usher in the calm, she almost sings.
She celebrates while my world falls away.
This blood. My lies.

Two hummingbirds danced around me
outside just now as I picked these herbs for you.
It means the hummingbird spirits blessed them
and the beginning of your journey
that we will soon announce at your moon ceremony.

I had forgotten the ceremony!

Stop, Mima! I shout in desperation.
Why does everyone have to know?
Celi! Don't you raise your voice at me!
Take a deep breath. Let the herbs soothe you.
An angry defiance continues to rise within me,
No, Mima! Don't you know anything about me?
Don't you know that I'd rather crawl into a cave
than have a stupid moon ceremony!
Celi, your moon will not be like mine.
You will not begin womanhood in doubt
in shame
but surrounded by the strength
of women in your community.
That is our way.
No it isn't. It is a way you've made up!
It is a way that we have to reclaim
so that we are not erased.
No!
It WILL happen whether you like it or not!

Mima leaves me to cry
sitting in a soup
of hummingbird herbs and rage.

CHRYSALIS

Mima walks back into the bathroom
holding a cup of tea, a pair of
clean underwear, and an assortment of
organic cotton pads and tampons.
I've cried so much my lungs
gasp uncontrollably for dashes of air
like extended hiccups.
I climb out of the tub
she wraps me in a large towel, mummy tight
like she did after the bath when I was a baby
and hugs me.

Celi, mi vida.
Mima's tone is sweet again.
We don't know if it hurts a butterfly
as it hatches from its chrysalis.
We see it struggle yes, but we know
that it will have a great reward.
In the end, it becomes a winged creature
more magical than when it started.

I press my head into her shoulder
and think about butterflies
I manage to grimace out a whimpy,
        Perdón, Mima.
My apology snuffed by the wet hair in my mouth.
I know, mija, I am sorry that we don't agree
but your body has come into the moon now
and we have to honor it.
She says as she brushes strands away,
How about we begin to prepare for it
and then see how you feel after?
I lay my forehead on her lips
with the littlest nod.

Then suddenly, Marco's on my mind
and my sloppy secrets finally rush out . . .
        I've been a creep to Marco.
        I went behind Marco's back
        and agreed to go to the movies with Iván
        after Iván made fun of Marco
        for being a xochihuah.

Surprised that I change the conversation
from me to Marco
and that I've sunk so low perhaps
Mima shakes her head and says,
I can't make that one better for you, mija.

TALKING DRUM

As I dress into my pajamas
Juju walks into our room
begins his banter of facts.
You know, you can't fold
a square in half more than seven times?
I've tried it with origami; it's impossible.
He's still a child and I envy what he doesn't know.

I can hear
the raindrop conga sound
of Papi's drums
coming from his studio.

Calling . . .

Juju's talking melts away.
I walk past him
out the door
toward the garage.

Papi is playing

a rumba guaguancó
I don't say a word
let my body begin to
answer the sounds of his drumming.
Papi welcomes me with a nod
turns up his playing
makes brighter sounds
round sounds
colored sounds
a timeless talking unlike
Mima's or Juju's.

I just dance.

Suddenly he switches rhythms
to a samba
and I fall deep in feet movement
a conga
and I climb spirit high from side to side
a bomba
and I twirl and mark my
beat with my arms
that Papi catches
effortlessly, in sync.

I don't see that
Mima and Juju

are both standing
at the door witnessing
with Papi
the closest I have ever
come to clarity
lighter and
as unstuck
as I could ever be.

Until I stop
too out of breath
to dance
anymore.

ANTICIPATION

Marco called me later
that evening on video chat.
The first time in so long.
He was worried about me.
Luckily, I've got the tablet again.

       Marco, I'm sorry, I say again, slowly.
       I went to the movies with Iván
       and his friends after he was mean to you.
I know. Juju told me.
       You knew?
Yeah, and I also know about
the solstice at the park. Aurora told me.
I ain't gonna lie. That hurt, Celi.
It's why I was so mad at you for so long.
       I was a real bum. I'm so sorry.
I reach out to the screen.
We try to simulate our handshake.
       Thanks for not hating me.
       You're a way better friend than I am.

Guess what? My mom wasn't all talk
she's really making me
have a moon ceremony, I surrender.

Whoa.

Mima says that I can invite a few friends
as a chance to learn about ceremonia
but I only want you to be there.
Will you come?

I don't know. It's for women only right?

She said it was okay because you're
a xochihuah with boy and girl energies
it's more sacred and stuff.

I guess she's right. You know what my dad told me?
He said that some Mexica priests
were xochihuah too
and were revered for it.
That shreds, que no?

See! It's perfect.

My dad also said that if I wanted to
we could do a Temazcal ceremonia for me.

You mean, like do a sweat lodge and pray all night kinda
thing.

Yeah, but for xochihuah. 'Cept we haven't figured out how it will
work.

That's hecka cool.

Marco shyly asks,
How's it feel to bleed?
I try to describe the wetness
the feeling like you are peeing but not
how the cotton pad that just sits there
collecting blood is really the strangest part.

It sort of trips me out
to think about when I'll get my moon.
      It's not as bad as it sounds. Don't get me wrong.
Not because of what you said, but because
for me, it'll be like going back
against what I've gained.
It will take me back to being
only the girl I used to be.
What if it erases my boyness?
I just want to continue to be me,
the Marco and Magda me, I mean.

      I hear ya.

I nod but I feel the opposite
about myself.
I don't say it out loud.
I'm done hurting his feelings.
I *do* want to go back to the girl
I used to be.

RECITAL

I wear an extra-absorbent pad
the next day for our recital.

Mima drops me off
one full block away from La Peña!
I can feel the bulk of the cotton
as I walk into the center
alone.

I see Iván come in early
even though I never invited him.

I march over without thinking
I smack him with words.

    I want you to know something.
    Marco is my friend.
    MY BEST FRIEND since we were babies
    and no one is going to make fun of him.
    I don't care how smart or funny you think you are!
Hi, Celi, nice to see you too.

His sarcasm stirs me for a second
with that crushy feeling again
but I shake it off quickly
because he makes me boil
and I keep going,

Marco's a xochihuah and
a reflection of the Creator, Ometeotl.
That Aztec calendar on your board
well, guess what?
The Mexica's number one creator spirit is Ometeotl
who's both male and female
just like Marco.
And if you are too stupid to see that
he's supposed to be honored and respected
because of this, then you have no
business having that calendar on
your board and no business
talking to me!

I walk away from Iván
my lips clenched
breathing fast
clasping my fists closed
in a knockout knot.

LAST QUARTER MOON

"Moon, I have come in with your song."

— *Apache puberty rite dance song*

PREPARATIONS

The day before the full moon
Mima and I build an altar
on the ground in the center of the garden.
Careful to honor the
Mexica four directions
we lay out the items . . .

In the East, the realm of Tlahuizlampa
the element of fire
where passion, illumination, and energy live
we lay candles.

Facing West, Cihuatlampa
that is the body of Mother Earth
where we are grounded
we offer leaves and moss.

To the South, in Huitzlampa
the element of water
where our cleansing, deep emotions, and dreams go
we place a bowl of water.

And North, Mictlampa
we revere the air
our spirits, the truth of our spoken word
and so we place a bell, a feather, a twig of sage.

The center pedestal
we reserve for statues of goddesses and spirits
from my Mexican side and my Caribbean side.
Mima asks me to arrange these statues as I wish.
I scatter them like the petals of a cempazuchitl flower
looking every which way.

> Tonantzin / Guadalupe — Mexica Earth Mother and
> Mexican Virgin Mary
> Coatlicue — Mexica mother of the cycle of life and death
> Yemayá — Yoruba spirit of the ocean
> Oyá — Yoruba spirit of the wind, of hurricanes
> Ochún — Yoruba spirit of sweet waters, fertility, and love
> Atabey — Taíno supreme goddess of fresh water and fertility
> Xochipilli / Xochiquetzal — Mexica flower prince and
> princess of the arts and all genders
> Ometeotl — Mexica creation spirit in divine balance

In the absolute center I place my favorite goddess:

> Coyolxauhqui — Mexica goddess of the moon
>> She lies on a disc, a woman fallen and broken
>> but a warrior who fought the god of war, the sun
>>> for honor.
>> Though she failed, she tried.
>> Coyolxauhqui comes back in bits

every single night
illuminating the sky little by little
until all of her broken pieces
become one.

As my last offering to my moon altar
I lay my first doll, Alma, inside an open gourd
then I add a flint, for protection
and a spool of thread to mend
her bird-print dress
I say goodbye beneath my breath
while Mima sprinkles her
with crystal dust
that feels like love.

Mima and I wrap four poles
one for each direction
with twine and red ribbons.
We hang strings of white lights
on trees and bushes
in what looks like a circle of light.

We talk about the new ceremonial white
dress I am going to wear for the night
my new sandals
and my grandmother Yeya's rebozo
that will fall from my shoulders
and surely touch the ground.

TOGETHER

Teresa and Marco arrive later to help us
but only Mima and Teresa
build the moon hut.
Marco and I watch as they
bring six bamboo poles together and
tie them at the top ends and extend them
so the figure looks like a tiny stick house.
They cover it with an ivory crochet bedspread
that belonged to my Yeya's grandmother
and looks like a beautiful spiderweb.
They decorate with evergreen branches and flowers.
This is where I will sit during ceremony.

We arrange straw mats on the grass
pillows and chairs for the elder women
who can't sit on the ground.

We wash and dry small glass jars
with their lids, then fill the jars with filtered water
and trim with a glittery ribbon.
These will be placed in front of each woman

to collect the light rays of the moon
so that we can drink
when our hearts need healing.

Marco and I collect kindling
twigs and newspaper for the fire pit.
Then place thirteen rocks around
the fire to represent the thirteen moons
that appear in a year.

Papi and Juju gather
caxixis, bells, maracas, and shakers
from Papi's collection for each of the women
because there will be no drums
allowed in this circle.

When I ask why,
Mima reminds me that Coyolxauhqui
has bells on her cheeks
and we honor her by only invoking
those sweet sounds.

A big pot of pozole
is slow cooking in the kitchen.
The smell that warms my belly
escapes our little house and finds
its way to the garden.

Tomorrow will be my first moon ceremony.
I look out into our garden
at the power we're gathering
then at Mima.
The feelings of strangeness
and nervousness that I've had
before today
peel away
as we work quietly
with our hands.

AT THE DOOR

The next evening
as guests arrive,
I can't stop biting my nails.
My aunties, my Yeya, and Chuyina
who've all come from LA are here.
The women from Mima and Teresa's women's circle
and Ms. Susana greet me
with the biggest hugs, which make
my anticipation rise
like warm bread in the oven.

When Marco and Teresa arrive
the small quivering of my skin begins to calm.
Marco is wearing pants AND a dress
pretty jacalosúchil flower beads around his neck
a xochihuah in the flesh.

The women magically whirl about
dressed in white outfits
and enjoy Mima's pozole dinner
when there's a knock on the door.

It's someone who wasn't invited.

Iván stands in the doorway.

When Marco and I near
      my face   reddens
my breath   shortens
      my eyes   dart
          from
Marco's too serious expression
          to
      Iván's cheeriness.

So I just close them and
open them when Iván says,

Hi, Celi, can I talk to you real quick?

Then he lifts his head at Marco
in a sort of friendly way.

I'm too embarrassed that he's here
that I don't say no.

LUNA REIGNS

I close the door behind me
walk away from the porch
down the steps toward the street.
When he follows
the flaming orange sun sets fast
behind us.

      What are you doing here?
I just want to say I'm sorry. But wait,
what's happening in there? You having a party?
I straighten up, take a deep breath, and say it,
      It's my moon ceremony.
Oooh, his eyebrows pop up.
Like the Aztec ceremony your mom talked about?
      Yes, and I gotta get back.

He bites his lower lip like
his nerves need to be held down
but then his words
come rushing out.
I'm really sorry if I made you mad, Celi. I'm not used

to being with people like Magda and I know she's
your friend and everything but it's just hard
to get, you know?

       You didn't have to be so mean to him?
Right, it's a him. She's a him. I mean.
See, I don't get it, but I want to.
Look, I just really like you. Like, "like" you.
And I know I've got to get Magda
or else I can't get close to you.

       Mar doesn't deserve how you've been
       regardless of me.
I know, you're right.

My panza begins to turn.
I'm having a hard time swallowing
     words and my own nerves rumble
the ebb of sparkling feelings lures me to him
      but then the flow of Marco's friendship
             pushes me back to shore.

Before I can respond
Iván gently reaches for my hand
     moves near
     says softly, *You look really pretty*, as he
       drops his head to the side
     and looks at me with will-you-forgive-me eyes.
He is so close

I can feel
the heat
of his face
near mine.

Celi, I'm sorry, he whispers.
                        In my ears his words are
            a never-ending tide
pulling against time   but not
because now the sun is gone
darkness creeps across the sky
            he leans in
                        could this be my first real kiss?

Then, in an instant, the
            sky
            swirls
                        and Luna pours into me.
I see Marco's joy
            our echo dancing and playing
                        that makes me soar
                                    like our two-birds-locking-and-flying
                                    handshake.
There can be no dance without music.

I remember also
my moon ceremony

the women in white
their hugs, the circle.

I remember that I am a butterfly now.

I turn my head away from Iván
and run up my stairs.

I am ready to fly.

A CIRCLE OF LIGHT

After the pozole
we move to the garden
where Luna shines
in all her brightness.
The fragrance of night-blooming jasmine surrounds us.
Yeya, our elder,
smudges each with copal incense smoke
before we enter the circle.

We look into the blazing fire in the center, hold hands.
Mima, Teresa, Ms. Susana, Yeya, my aunts, Chuyina,
other women from Mima's women's group,
Marco and I.

      My stomach does somersaults.

In Mima's welcome, she asks us all
to say thank you in the Mexica language, Nahuatl.
     Tlazohcamati!

Grateful first to Ometeotl
to our ancestors
to Mother Earth
and especially to Grandmother Moon
for which we have all dressed in white.
She acknowledges that we stand
on Ohlone land and honors
the indigenous people of Oakland.
She honors all present
the elders who no longer bleed
those who bleed now
those who don't bleed
and those who still haven't bled.
She asks us to say out loud
the one thing we are grateful for
at the same time.

Though my palms are sweaty
as I hold Marco's right hand with my left
I say I am grateful for my body.
I can hear Marco has said the same.

Mima has us turn
to each of the four directions
to thank each for their gifts
but we also look down to the earth and finally up to the sky
to receive a blessing from the entire universe.

We know to turn our bodies because Teresa blows
into a conch shell the size of a melon
and releases its bellowing sound into the air.

I walk slowly into
the brightly lit moon hut
and don't know
on which of the two pillows to sit.
My heartbeat races
like a horse inside my body.

Without warning
Mima sings a song loudly that is
by the elder, Abuela Margarita,

> *Luna llena, luna llena*
> *Lléname, lléname de amor*
> *Luna llena, luna llena*
> *Lléname, lléname de amor.*

All the women shake their rattles
when she is done.

Tonight we are here to welcome the coming
of Celestina Rivera's first moon blood
her moon within
under the light of this ancient full moon
by the sacred fire
with all of the divine feminine energy

in the center of our altar and in this circle.

I look around at all of the women and
their eyes
are all
on
me!

Instead of wanting to bite my nails
or hide like I thought I would
I feel a warm air travel
from my feet
to my chest
and rush
to the top
of my head.

And we are also gathered in this circle
to celebrate a sacred member of our community,
Marco Magdalena Sánchez, who today
we publicly honor for being a xochihuah,
the one who bears flowers
who is a reflection of our Creator, Ometeotl,
and holds both the female energy and the male energy
in harmony.

We believe that our Mexica ancestors knew
when two energies came together
as one, it could only be considered sacred.
And as we reclaim and rebuild our traditions
we also create this space for you to be blessed
by your community.

I turn to Marco
sitting cross-legged
next to my hut
and his mouth
is open in surprise.

Teresa walks over to Marco
helps him to his feet and moves him
over to my moon hut
and signals him to sit
on the empty pillow next to me.

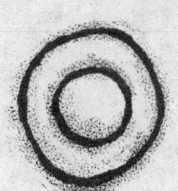

I reach out and hug Marco
our eyes begin to water
but we fight back our tears.
Our mothers sit on either side
of the hut that is *now ours*
as they take turns
leading the different rituals.

THE CLEANSING

We both stand in front of two tin basins
filled with agua florida, flower essence water
that Yeya's prepared for us.
She's mixed
      jacalosúchil blossoms and roses
      plus, dragon's blood blooms, ruda flowers
      and night-blooming jasmine.

Each of our mothers dips their hands
in the water and lightly brushes the water
on our feet, our hands, our clothes, our necks, our heads.
This is our cleansing, our freeing.

Yeya prays: *May this sacred water wash away*
your fears, negativity, and sadness. May it leave you
feeling inspired and ready to dream on your life's journey.

THE XOCHITL RITUAL

Each woman takes a flower, a xochitl, from the
center altar and places or pins it in
our hair, clothes, around our ankles and wrists.

Now Teresa prays: *May these flowers, symbols of
your blooming into adulthood, help you continue to blossom
into the person you are meant to be. Marco Xochihuah,
especially, these flowers are your beauty, your strength,
your perseverance and purpose.*

I turn and pin a xochitl over
Marco's chest
I understand that he's never
had a secret locket at all
but an open, flowering heart.

OMETEOTL

Mima guides me back to the hut
and Marco stays standing.
Teresa in front of him
holds his hands while
she stares into his eyes.

In an almost chant-like tone she calls:
Tonight, I honor you, Marco Xochihuah,
for the balance and duality that you are.
Two energies in one body
like the day and night
sadness and joy
death and life.
There cannot be one without the other.

As a reflection of Ometeotl
you are fluidity in motion.
You may bleed like a woman
and you may move as a man in the world
as you have chosen to do now.
Wherever you decide to thrive

remember that you are perfection in the crossroads.
No one can derail you from who you are
not even yourself because you
have been made this way by the Creator.
I honor your wisdom.
I honor your power.
I honor your strength.
I love you.
Tlazohcamati, xochihuah.
Tlazohcamati, Ometeotl.

Teresa then steps back and asks Marco
to speak.

> Ever since I was little,
> I felt like there was more to me
> than what people saw.
> I didn't know how to
> explain it until I learned
> about the xochihuah and Ometeotl.
> Duality seems like
> me on some days
> but most days, I feel more
> boy than girl.
> To be honest, I'm still trying to figure
> out where I'll end up — a boy, a girl, or both —
> but I can say this:
> I feel lucky to have

this spiritual path to guide me.
I just want my family
and friends to understand me
to accept me for who I am
and who I will be.

Teresa then places a necklace around his neck
on which hangs a charm — the symbol of Ometeotl
she kisses and hugs him tightly.
The rattles shake loudly
with tears and yelps of joy.

FIRST BLOOD RITUAL

Mima turns to me
holds her hands out so that
I join her near the altar.
She clasps my hands
her black eyes a soothing balm over me
and speaks:
A full moon for many cultures
is a time for magic
for healing
for rituals.
Indigenous ancestors created a space
called moon time
where women
could replenish, create, dream, and rest
when they bled.

Our ancestors believed it to be supernatural
that women could bleed for so many days
and not die

then give life.
And so the community honored and respected
these days for every woman.
With this ritual, we honor you, Celi, because
you are now part of this ancestry
a lineage of life-givers.
We are here to hold you as you
leave your childhood behind
and become a new moon, a woman.

She places a necklace around my neck
and explains that each black clay bead
marks a day in the twenty-nine-day lunar cycle
separated by moonstones for each
of the eight phases of the moon.

She continues,
Tonight you will offer
your first blood to Mother Earth, Tonantzin,
who will keep your power and transform it
to good soil and new life that we need to live.

Mima hands me a purse
that holds a little piece of cloth
stained brownish red.
She announces that this is my
first blood she collected and cut from

my underwear in the hamper.
Then she asks me to wash
the cotton cloth in
my basin with agua florida.
The water turns a pale red with my blood.

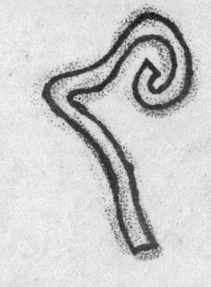

I don't blush or turn away.
My locket unhinges.
I'm in awe by how
the red-tinged silk of the water
easily swishes
through my fingers.

Then Mima asks me
to dig a small pit in the ground
with a hand shovel and gives me cut flowers
to line the rim of the hole like a wreath.
The smell of freshly turned dirt
fills my nose with a lulling safety.
Then Mima asks me to pour
this water into the pit and say:
  Madre Tierra, Tonantzin,
  please receive my first blood,
  my first moon.
Then, I add without Mima asking,
  Tlazohcamati, Tonantzin.
  Gracias, Mima, amigas, y mi amifriend.

Thank you, Grandmother Moon.
Tlazohcamati, mi Luna.
May the circle never be broken.

On my last word
the rattles shake loudly.
The sound shatters my locket.
I am as open as the moon.
I look up to see Luna's moonbeams
circle all of the people that surround me:
Mima, Teresa, Yeya, Marco too.
Luna is dancing tonight.
Translucent light glistens
around my hands
my first blood
the earth I've fed
the flowers hanging in my hair
in my new woman's womb
and finds a place to rest
in my heart.

MIDNIGHT LIGHT

It is nearly midnight
when I come in from the garden
and settle into bed.
I try not to wake Juju.

My skin still tingles.
The stories and advice
every woman
shared with me
about their moons
      about being a woman
stir in my mind.

Secrets
that could only have been given
      to me now
      after my own moon.
They fill my locket
and I feel it overflow.

I open my jar of moonbeam water

take a sip and I notice
Luna's rays have followed me in.

In the middle of the room
we flutter together
my arms outstretched
longer now
and winged.

I look into the beautiful dark
and sway with Luna's moonbeams
as we dance into the night.

El Fin

AUTHOR'S NOTE

Dear Reader,

Throughout history, there have been as many ways to connect with the moon as there have been people. How could we not marvel at the closest celestial body to the earth? How could we not feel how she affects us, when we pay attention? The moon faithfully shows us her many phases month after month, even in brightly lit urban areas, like Oakland, where we don't always see stars.

For those of us who menstruate, our natural connection to the moon is undeniable. Our menstrual cycles mirror the moon's own twenty-nine-day cycle. People in many cultures across the globe have honored this connection and practiced ceremonies and rituals (both big and small) for thousands of years. The modern-day Western ideas so prevalent in the United States today, which say that our bodies and our menstruations are dirty, to be feared or hated, are but one small piece of the human experience throughout history.

In the Americas, much of the knowledge of this natural connection has been lost, erased, or went underground as its peoples were conquered and forced to take on the customs of their colonizers. Many of the oral histories, passed down by indigenous women, tell us that our moon cycle is something beautiful and worth celebrating and honoring. How moon ceremonies in particular have been performed by women with indigenous blood has changed and continues to change with each generation, as we migrate, mix cultures, experiences, and knowledge. What I've shared in this book is *one* such way that was inspired by my Mexican indigenous roots but that also combines Caribbean traditions (as Celi is bicultural Puerto Rican/Mexican, and multiracial Indigenous, African, and European), plus modern-day elements, my intuition, and ideas. There are other ways Xicanas (girls and women in the US with Mexican origins, pronounced *shee-kah-nahs*) practice coming of age rituals too, like Xilonen (*shee-lów-nen*), which involves up to a year of preparations and is rooted in Aztec dance. What unites us is a reverence for coming of age rituals, our ancestral connection to the moon, and an insistence that the practice of honoring the moon's connection to our beautiful bodies survives.

One way to ensure this survival of knowledge is to keep it close within communities, to avoid adoption or misinterpretation by outsiders. Another is to share it more widely. With deep respect to the former and the act of resistance it represents, I chose to write my version of a Xicana moon ceremony because I believe the forgetting, erasing, and lack of access to this information has contributed to the negative ways many Xicanas see menstruation. In my view, these risks are more damaging than the risks of exposure. For the young Xicanas and Latinas with similar histories out there, I want to ensure you know that traditions like these exist and belong to you. I want you to understand your bodies and your ancestry more fully. I know I wish I had as a young girl.

Similarly, it was precolonial indigenous ideas that inspired me to write a genderfluid character like Marco. As a cisgender Xicana, disappointed with the often negative way that some in my community view and treat gender-expansive people, my intention was to offer an alternative. Mesoamericans had a broader understanding of gender and some evidence shows us that xochihuah (*sho-chee-wah*) were more often seen through a sacred lens, with respect. Though we can't be certain if it was otherwise, my challenge to my community is to use some of this ancestral wisdom as a guide to embrace xochihuah, and to reject intolerance. To young gender-expansive readers, please know that within these pages you are seen, you have a place, and you are held in love.

Finally, we must understand that though all of us are connected to the moon and our ancestors, the practices shown here are not necessarily meant to be taken as one's own. I encourage you, reader, to look into your own ancestry to see what has been done. And if those traditions do not honor you, then use that source as inspiration to correct a wrong and create something meaningful for you and the girls, women, and gender-expansive people in your community.

There are a couple of additional offerings that you'll find here. The first is a wonderful poem, "A Flower Song for Maidens Coming of Age." Writer, translator, and scholar on Mesoamerican cultures and languages David Bowles translated into English this poem that was originally written in 1440, before European contact in Mexico, and found in a collection of Yucatec Maya poems called *Songs of Dzitbalché 7*. When I first read "Flower Song," I was moved to tears, not only because this was a huge opening in my understanding of myself as a woman and my ancestral cultures, but also because it validated this book. "Flower Song" is the only Mesoamerican precolonial written description of a moon ceremony in existence *and* it is written in verse, just like this book. When I read it, though it was Maya and not Mexica, I felt as if the ancestors had reached across the centuries to bless this book in both content and form. David Bowles has graciously allowed us to reprint his English translation here. It is my every hope that you feel its blessing too.

The other offering you will find here is a moon calendar, drawn by the amazing cover artist Joe Cepeda. The easiest way to begin to learn how you are connected to the moon is by charting how you feel throughout the months. You can trace or copy this moon calendar onto a clean sheet of paper and use it to see how your feelings and your body change throughout the different phases of the moon. If you do it month to month, you will likely begin to see patterns, a wonderful ongoing choreography of your very own dance with the moon.

May all of these offerings find a place inside your locket. May you find comfort, healing, understanding, and curiosity about your body, your gender, your art, your ancestry, your community, your beauty—whatever is inside your heart. May this inspire you to not fear but to love the power that is within you. May this courage help you to be proud and to speak your truth so that we may change negative ideas that would rather see you silent or ashamed of who you are. May all of this, dear reader, ring out into the world for the strengthening of us all.

With love,

Aida

"A FLOWER SONG FOR MAIDENS COMING OF AGE"

The beautiful, beautiful moon
Has risen above the woods,
Tracing her bright path
Across the heavens.
Suspended, she pours light
Upon the woods,
The earth entire.

A breeze blows sweetly,
Carrying perfumed scents.
The moon reaches her zenith—
Her glow silvering the world.
Joy sings out
Within every good soul.

We reach the center,
The womb of the forest:

Utter stillness.
No one will see
What we have come to do.

We have brought flowers:
Lol nikte—frangipani blossoms,
Lol chukum—dragon's blood blooms,
Lol u ul—dog jasmine petals.

We have brought copal incense
And wild bamboo.
A tortoise shell
And crystal dust.

We have brought new cotton thread
And gourds for our spindles.
A large, lovely flint
and a counterweight.
New needlework
and a sacrificial bird.

New sandals, too . . .
Everything new,
Even the thongs we use
To tie our hair back

So the old woman,
Teacher and guide,
Can anoint our necks with nectar
As she instructs us
In the ways of women.

"We stand at the heart
Of the forest,
Beside the stone pool,
Waiting for Venus,
The smoking star,
To glimmer
Above the trees.
Remove your clothes.
Let down your hair.
Bask in the moonlight,
Naked as the day of your birth,
Virgins,
Maidens,
Women."

(*Songs of Dzitbalché 7*)
Translated by David Bowles

ACKNOWLEDGMENTS

Gracias hasta la luna . . .

The Moon Within was born because of the sacrifices, lessons, and blessings given to me by an intricate cosmology of people and spirits. I am deeply grateful to each ancestor, each elder, each teacher, each writer, each dear one whose magic held me or challenged me but ultimately lifted me so that I could write this book. This work is because of you and for you.

To Marietta Zacker, not only my agent but true kindred spirit and homegirl, gracias del alma for your belief in my work and for being a brilliant guiding light. I am beyond grateful to my wildly gifted editor, Nick Thomas, whose laser beam mind and open spirit found my work in the rubble at the SCBWI-LA conference and to my amazement became the greatest ally, counselor, advocate, and loving protector of the truth within these pages. Biggest love to Kait Feldmann, magical editor of my picture book, *Jovita Wore Pants: The Story of a Revolutionary Fighter*, and feminista sister who went to bat hard for me, and whose fire and light inspire me to stay true to my vision. Arthur A. Levine, it humbles me to no end that you trust, stand with, and have fought for my voice and choices, thank you! Gracias to the incomparable Joe Cepeda, who understood the essence of this story so perfectly that to see his first sketch of the cover left me breathless. Lunar thanks to my stellar accuracy readers whom I will call "p/madrinxs of the moon" for blessing this book with your expert wisdom: Mason J., Dr. Lara Medina, Yolanda Coyolxauhqui Valenzuela, Elise McMullen-Ciotti, Parrish Turner, Kyle Lukoff, and especially, David Bowles, who led me to his translation of a very special gift—"Flower Song," the last surviving piece of precolonial literature about moon ceremonies in the Americas. Warm thanks to Erin Casey, Nancy Gallt, and the Gallt Zacker Literary Agency team for being so amazing to me.

Thank you to my wonderfully supportive book-loving family at Scholastic—Weslie Turner, whose woke analysis contributed to the strength of this book; to wonderful designer and artist, Maeve Norton, thank you for making this book so gorgeous; Lizette Serrano, weaver of book dreams come true, thank you; and the dynamic Emily Heddleson, Danielle Yadao, and Jasmine Miranda for all your team's support. To my fabulous publicist, Crystal McCoy; to Tracy van Straaten, Ellie Berger, Jody Stigliano, Yesenia Corporan, and Ann Marie Wong; and the warm and generous US Scholastic sales team, to whom I had the honor of meeting, thank you for helping my book reach more children than I ever imagined. Special thanks to Andrea Davis Pinkney, whose book *The Red Pencil* first inspired me to return to my origins as a poet as a way to tell this story.

Gracias de todo corazón to my amiga, Diana Perez, for your unconditional and enthusiastic support of my writing since we were mocosa seventeen year olds, and for nursing this story with so much tenderness and plot doctora skill; to Yolanda Coyolxauhqui Valenzuela, moon priestess and dearest friend whose astrological and spiritual wisdom first sprouted and sustains my love of the moon; to my amigas adoradas, remarkable writers and artists among you: Maria Elena Fernandez, Vickie Vertiz, Maris Curran, Adia Millett, Isabel Garcia Gonzalez, Victoria Delgadillo, Jamaica Itule Simmons, Joe Loya, Raul Balthazar, Norma Liliana Valdez, Yaccaira Salvatierra, Leticia Del Toro, Sandra Garcia Rivera, Susan Marchiona, Elizabeth Hansen, Roberto Lovato, Jesus Sierra, Michlene Cotter, Shefali Shah, Raquel Pinderhughes, Conceição Damasceno and Yamile Saied Méndez, for providing the best feedback for the book or for seeing me through many meltdowns when I was buried in motherhood, afraid of writing, and for listening—truly listening—and loving me through it until I remembered that I was an artist too. To my dearest artist friends, both children and their adults (so many they would fill an entire book), in the LA and Bay Area Xicanx, Puerto Rican bomba, Brazilian, Cuban, Latin jazz, world, folk, and hip-hop dance, music, writing and art communities: Thank you for making the arts our family's lifeblood.

Cosmic thanks to my IBPOC literary cannon who have dug our stories out from the margins and paved a way with your magic words. The greatest gratitude for your reading and generous blurbs and support, Juan Felipe Herrera (trailblazing cloud poet and enduring muse), Margarita Engle, Olugbemisola Rhuday-Perkovich, David Bowles, and Naheed H. Senzai (who was the first ever to professionally read and encourage these pages). I will be forever grateful to Daria Peoples and Leah Henderson for opening the door and my eyes to the world of publishing in such a selfless and loving manner. To my fantastic Las Musas collective (Hilda Burgos, Jennifer J.C. Cervantes, Tami Charles, Ann Davila Cardinal, Natasha Davis, Mia Garcia, Isabel Ibañez Davis, Tehlor Kay Mejia, Ana Meriano, Nina Moreno, Maya Motayne, Claribel Ortega, Emma Otheguy, Kristina Perez, Laura Pohl, NoNieqa Ramos, Michelle Ruiz Keil, Yamile Saied Méndez, and Mary Louise Sanchez), I am so grateful to be on this journey with you. Thank you to my imprint siblings for our sweet AALB/Scholastic bond—Mike Yung, Kelly Yang, and Tony Piedra. Thank you to Latinx in Kidlit, Latinx in Publishing and POC in Publishing for the selfless work of opening and keeping the gates opened for us. Gracias to the amazing Marcela Landres, who gave me such generous and spot-on strategies to become a professional author; to Christina Garcia and Carolina de Robertis and all the beautiful writers at Las Dos Brujas Workshop 2017, I love being a bruja with you. To La Lunada Literary Lounge, thank you for being a steadfast refuge of words for me. To my sister writers at Community of Writers at Squaw Valley and at the magical Hedgebrook, thank you for holding space for my pain. To Hillary Homzie and Mira Reisberg at Children's Book Academy, whose teachings helped me revise my first draft of this manuscript; to Lin Oliver and all the SCBWI writers and workshop leaders for offering their best. To the wonderful Oakland Public Library librarians and staff: Derrick DeMay, Annabelle Blackman, Miriam Medow, Mahasin Jullanar, Isela Anaya, and Pete Villaseñor, who provided the perfect book world for a hibernating writer and her book-hungry kids. A most special thanks to Isabel Shazam, Roberto Miguel, Patti O'Reiley, and the Sonoma Conservatory of Dance— the first to believe that moonbeams and girls were meant to dance together.

All of the gracias in the world to my source, mi mami bella, Maria Isabel Salazar Viramontes, for teaching me about the power in herbal medicine, for your will to live a full and beautiful life in the face of tragedy and for loving me, mas; to my father, Fidel Rafael Salazar, who showed me what it is to hold immigrant dreams close and never let go; to my siblings, Isabel, Rafael, Edith, Veronica, Angelica, Belinda, and siblings-in-law Nelida, Carlos, and Tom—each of you are so singularly vital to the beating of my heart—thank you hermanas y hermanos for everything; to my nieces and nephews Sammy, Jonathan, Janelle, Mikey, Kristen, CJ, and Miley for allowing me to be witness to the wonder of your lives and for fortifying my resolve to write stories for youth. To my abuel@s, ti@s, and prim@s, some whom have recently gone into the realm of the ancestors, I hold you close no matter how far I go. To the beautiful and wild Puerto Rican and Cape Verdean family I married into, thank you for sharing your sabor y amor with me.

Most importantly, to my angel, Amaly, and my living children João and especially Avelina—the brilliant inspiration for this story—thank you, amores, for trusting me with the sanctity of mothering you, and for your art-filled lives and blossoming that have taught me to reach deep into the part of me that holds love, pain, and the hopes for a better world, and then to sing it all from my pen. Finally, I offer loving gratitude to my encanto, John, for rescuing me, sustaining me, delighting me, and loving me like no one ever. It is such a blessing to dance in this world with you.

AFTER WORDS™

AIDA SALAZAR'S

The Moon Within

CONTENTS

About the Author
Q&A with Aida Salazar
Discussion Questions
The History of Bomba
My Moon Within

After Words™ guide by Jessica N. Harold

About the Author

Aida Salazar is a writer, arts advocate, and mother whose writings explore issues of identity and social justice. She was born in Mexico and grew up in Southeast Los Angeles where she spent many days sitting in little puddles of water on cement believing she was in the ocean.

When asked about the importance of her debut middle grade novel *The Moon Within*, Aida said: "In many ways, I wrote it for myself, now that I have reclaimed menstruation's power, to heal and break free from the damaging narrative that I too had internalized during my own coming of age and beyond." Her forthcoming novel in verse, *Land of the Cranes*, follows a little girl who stands hopeful and strong despite being caged in a US immigration detention facility. Aida will make her picture book debut in *Jovita Wore Pants: The Story of a Revolutionary Fighter*, illustrated by Molly Mendoza, a story based on the life of her distant great aunt, Jovita Valdovinos. Her short story, "By the Light of the Moon," was adapted for the Sonoma Conservatory of Dance and premiered in April 2016. It is the first Xicana-themed ballet in history.

Aida received an MFA in Writing from the California Institute of the Arts, and her writings have appeared in publications such as *Huffington Post*, *Huizache Magazine*, and *Women and Performance: Journal of Feminist Theory*. She is also a founding member of Las Musas, the first collective of debut/sophomore Latinx authors in US children's literature.

She currently lives in Oakland, CA, with her husband, Latin jazz musician John Santos, and homeschools one of her two fiery artist children. To learn more about Aida and her work, visit aidasalazar.com.

Q&A with Aida Salazar

Q: *How did you first get interested in writing? Was it something you always wanted to do, even as a child?*

A: I fell in love with books in the fifth grade at Loma Vista Elementary in Maywood, CA. My teacher, Mr. Clark, a well-dressed and inspiring teacher, was the first to ever give me a novel to read as an independent reader. It was such a foreign thing for me because in my home, I received the power of story from my Mexican family through the way they offered memories, boleros, jokes, tongue twisters, and through the fun ways we spoke Spanglish. But, when I was given a book to read just for myself, it was as if an entire universe of joy opened up for me. I read book after book in his classroom and when I was done, I read those I could borrow from the library. Mr. Clark also introduced me and his students to choral singing because he was a great piano player, to history through the slide images of wonderful pieces of art he photographed in his world travels, to visual art making through projects that reflected our readings. He taught through the arts. I'd never loved learning so much.

The day I graduated from fifth grade, the school awarded me the Johnston Award for academic excellence. As a graduation gift, Mr. Clark gave me two things—a pen and a book. The pen was a Parker pen, a weighted metal instrument which included two replaceable ink cartridges. I'd never owned anything so fancy. The book was Shel Silverstein's *Where the Sidewalk Ends*—a book filled with the most hilarious poetry and illustrations. If I ever verbalized I wanted to be a writer in fifth grade, I don't remember it. I only remember loving words. After elementary school, I remember writing only the most special things with the pen, writing that was trying to be like art and which rhymed like Shel Silverstein's work. I've long lost that beloved pen but *Where the Sidewalk Ends* sits on my bookshelf though tattered and stained because I've read it hundreds of times.

It dawned on me recently that Mr. Clark's gifts were what planted the seeds of writing in my imagination though I didn't realize it at the time. My debut book, as you know, is a novel of poems and was originally written in long hand with a pen! I like to believe that Mr. Clark must have seen in me a possibility that I didn't see. What he did was set me in motion, like when one sets intentions on the new moon, and the publication of my own book, *The Moon Within*, is the completion of that cycle, the celebration of the full moon of my writing life. One day, I hope to find Mr. Clark and thank him.

Q: *When did you first see yourself reflected in a book?*
A: It wasn't until I was in my first year in college in a Latinx literature course when I read *Woman Hollering Creek* by Sandra Cisneros that I saw myself, my family, and my community inside the pages of a book. It was a magnificent awakening, but also sad on some level because it took 17 years! I had gone my entire elementary school, middle school, and high school life never seeing anyone whose experiences remotely reflected mine. Luckily, in this course I read about a dozen beautiful novels after Sandra's that broadened my awakening. Not only did I see myself reflected but I was able to believe that if these authors could write about us, then all of the scribbling I did with that Parker pen could someday be published. I could be a writer too.

Q: *What does Oakland represent, in this story and for you?*

A: My family and I live a rich cultural life in Oakland, and I wanted to show readers its beauty. The African American community along with the diverse immigrant populations in the San Francisco Bay Area are part of what defines the cultural landscape here. There are wonderful cultural centers and organizations that offer classes and performances that make the arts feel very alive. La Peña Cultural Center, for instance, is a real place where my family goes regularly. The arts are often the way many communities can preserve and celebrate their traditions but also make statements about how they have been hurt by forces like racism, sexism, homophobia and transphobia, or poverty and trauma. Without the arts, Oakland would be a very different place. Though bigotry exists even in the best of circumstances, the San Francisco Bay Area is more welcoming than most parts of the country of the LGBTQIA+ communities. We are lucky to have paid witness to the thriving of many of our friends. I know this is an experience many people in the Bay Area also live and cherish and I wanted to show how we experience the arts, gender expansive acceptance, and moon ceremonies as beautiful practices for children and families.

Q: *Celi's family is very in touch with ancestral traditions. Were they also a part of your own upbringing? And what do you think can be gained from this knowledge in our modern lives?*

A: As a child, my family practiced many cultural traditions that were connected to our Catholic faith. Rituals like mass on Sundays, baptisms, first holy communions, quinceañeras, and so many others were part of my upbringing. When I went to college and began to study our history, I realized that I didn't know any of the pre-Columbian spiritual rituals rooted in my indigenous ancestry because they had been destroyed during colonization (the time when Europeans came to the Americas and enforced their religion and practices). This is true for many Mexicans and those native to the Americas. Even though many of us have large quantities of indigenous blood, our ancestral indigenous tribes, our connection to the practices of this ancestry have been erased, or silenced, and destroyed. There are many making great efforts to try to find and revive these traditions, like Mima in *The Moon Within* and like me. But also, there are many indigenous communities in the Americas who resisted colonization and have maintained their indigenous ways and languages and are vital today. Those of us hungry for this knowledge learn from them, the oral traditions they keep alive, but also from findings about our archaeological sites, and some from the codices—the last surviving books about indigenous Mesoamerica before and during the conquest. The codex *Songs of Dzitbalché* is from where we found the special poem, "A Flower Song for Maidens Coming of Age." There are some traces of our indigenous roots in our daily lives, however. You can find them woven into our stories, into our languages, in the way many continue to make tortillas by hand, or use a pestle and mortar to make the most delicious chiles, in the medicinal use of herbs, in the rebozos we still wear, and in our faces. We revive and reclaim traditions that were lost to try to uplift ourselves and our community. We do so to heal from the great hurt and loss that colonization left behind.

Q: *Is Celi based on anyone in your life?*

A: Celi was inspired by my daughter. I had not yet read a story about a bi-cultural, multi-racial Latina like her in any book and so I decided to write it. In fact, I used my entire family and life in Oakland as a sketch for the characters and setting. My husband is a percussionist, I am a practitioner of herbal medicine, and my son really did have open-heart surgery (and is a fast talker). My daughter dances bomba, bites her nails, is a secret keeper, and did have a moon ceremony. However, everything about the plot was fictional. My daughter welcomed her moon ceremony with open arms unlike Celi because we attended moon ceremonies for other girls in our community. It was something we respected and celebrated together. For this story, however, I thought it would be interesting to write a character who didn't welcome her changes and feared the thought of a moon ceremony. I wanted Celi to reluctantly discover the beauty and magic that happens during the tender time of puberty and how powerful it is when based on ancestral traditions that celebrate our bodies, honor our natural cycles, and our natural connection to the moon.

Q: *Do you have any advice for young people who want to write?*

A: It is important to read as much and as widely as you can. There is so much richness to find within the pages of any book but don't forget to listen. Careful listening will deepen anything you write. Listen to the stories of elders, to songs, jokes, tongue twisters, to conversations happening around you. Pay close attention to the many details that make life joyful, or sad, or boring, or interesting. All of this will fill your writer's mind and heart and will make its way into your writing. Any time you get your words out is practice—even if you write on napkins or in a journal, or on your phone. Sometimes it will take a long time to surface, but be patient and gentle with yourself. The beauty and the truth inside you will come as you practice and remember what you've read and heard.

Q: *Why was it important to include characters like Marco and Iván in this book?*

A: This book was written for blooming menstruators of all genders. I wanted the blossoming of the main character (girlhood into womanhood) to mirror the blossoming of her best friend into his genderfluidity, a xochihuah. Each blossoming is a universe apart but similar in its impact and understanding of their own coming of age.

Most of the people who menstruate are girls or women, and sometimes menstruators are gender expansive. Though I don't go into Marco's specific experience with menstruation and only really hint at it because I could not authentically tell that story as a cisgender woman, I wanted to include in the book the notion that bodies, regardless of gender, can and do bleed monthly so as to expand understanding for readers that menstruation is not only a woman's experience. Also, I included La Chuyina, the transfeminine character, to affirm that womanhood too, is not dependent on bleeding.

What I could speak to was how clumsy and wrong we can be when we aren't good allies to our gender expansive friends. I sought to challenge readers, my community in particular, in our often-bigoted views. Iván represents this when he makes fun of Marco for presenting as male. It is hard for us to break down old ways of thinking. I used Mesoamerican philosophy to help us remember that our precolonial ideas of gender were more fluid than the binary that is dominant today. I saw an opportunity to show how one community used a different approach, one that was grounded in Mexica spirituality, to show compassion and respect for gender expansiveness.

Iván also represents a multi-racial and multi-cultural person, like Celi. Many children of mixed heritage live in Oakland. I find it beautiful how they navigate multiple cultures—sometimes with a sense of wonder and pride, and sometimes with neglect or shame and every feeling in between. It's complicated and certainly isn't always seamless given so much discussion over racial and cultural purity that is happening today. Through those characters, I wanted to show this negotiation, how they deal with these fusions. I wanted to show readers what it might look like for someone to celebrate and embrace all of who they are. Similarly, I wanted to show the intersectionality of Marco's identity as a genderfluid Mexican that happens to be in love with playing bomba (an Afro-Puerto Rican form of music). It was important to show readers that we could be queer and Mexican, Black Puerto Rican Mexican, and Black and Mexican. The range of identities is part of the beauty of who they are, and serves to strengthen and not weaken them.

Q: *What do you hope readers take away from Celi's story?*
A: I hope boys, girls, and genderfluid children of color see themselves represented well in this book. I hope that it reaches the child who is unsure of or ashamed of their menstruation or who they are, or where their gender lies. I hope *The Moon Within* teaches them to feel empowered by the beauty of their bodies and the beauty of their own transformations.

Discussion Questions

How does Celi feel about her body's changes? How does Mima see those changes? In what ways are their views similar and in what ways are they different?

Teresa asks Celi to help Marco with his transition "as a xochihuah safe and loving within the community." What are some ways she helps him feel safe and loved?

Iván says, "I don't get it, but I want to." Why does Celi respond the way she does? What advice would you give Iván?

During the moon ceremony, what is the significance of the items placed on the altar, carried by people in the circle, and placed on Celi and Marco? And what is the significance of the words shared by Mima, Teresa, and the elder Yaya?

Celi experiences some transformative moments at La Peña, Lake Merritt, and visiting family in Los Angeles. Describe how communities and events at each of those places influence Celi.

How does music, drumming, and dancing described in the book mirror the developments in Celi and Marco's friendship?

Marco says, "I just want to continue to be me, the Marco and Magda me," and Celi tells Iván, "Marco's a xochihuah and a reflection of the Creator, Ometeotl." How have characters like Teresa and Papi described Marco's transition? What is your understanding of how Marco self-identifies?

What are some words you would use to describe Celi and Marco's friendship? How did that change over the course of the book?

(Discussion questions by Dr. Carla España, Bilingual Education Clinical Doctoral Lecturer at Hunter College, The City University of New York; Educator Collaborative K-12 Literacy Professional Development Fellow)

The History of Bomba

Bomba is a form of percussion-heavy music born and developed in Puerto Rico. Its roots can be traced back to Spanish colonization. The Spanish captured and brought many people from West Africa to work plantations on the American continents as free labor. Some of these Africans had traded and fought with one another, and others did not even speak the same language. One commonality that brought these people together in the face of hardship was remembering cultural traditions from their homeland, especially music. For many enslaved Africans in North and South America, dance and music became forms of communication, as well as avenues of self-expression and remembering the home they could not return to. Across the Americas, many different forms of African music and rhythmic dance transformed into something entirely new and different, like blues in the USA. Bomba is uniquely Puerto Rican, with both Spanish and indigenous Taíno influence.

As Africans were bought and sold and moved around on the island, the knowledge of bomba went with them. Different regions began to add their own take on the style, which eventually developed into new varieties. Soon bomba was used for virtually every occasion like marriages and holidays among the enslaved Africans and became an escape from the suffering and horrors of slavery in Puerto Rico. Bomba also developed as a means of dissent against slave owners. Many rebellions were organized with the help of bomba to relay messages across different plantations.

In bomba, there is one main drummer, the primo, who creates a dialogue with a dancer through rhythm in a song, sung by a cantor. There is also the buleadors who create a circle around the primo and follow the primo's rhythm. The circle, or batey, is where the dancer enters to begin their musical conversation with the primo. The two then begin piquetes, improvising with one another. They are often encouraged by the buleadors and audience. Many bomba songs are still well-known in Afro-Puerto Rican communities.

The word "bomba" comes from the name of the drum used, usually a repurposed barrel that merchants had used to transport goods. The other two instruments typically used come from the Taínos: cuás (wooden sticks) and maracas. The primo drum is smaller and less wide so its sound stands out more with the dancer's piquetes. People usually wear white clothes for bomba dance—shirts, pants, skirts and petticoats, hats, and turbans—in the same style worn in colonial Puerto Rico. The flounces of a dancer's skirt and petticoat are meant to fly, spin, and twirl in time to the beat of the drums.

Bomba music as a genre became popularized in the 1940s and 1950s, fused with other regional genres and performed around the world. But no matter its growth and development in the music industry, more traditional styles are still practiced. La Peña Cultural Center was founded in response to the 1973 coup in Chile that resulted in the military dictatorship and remains a popular institution in California for bomba classes and performances.

Bomba is an expansive and unique dance and music that remains an important part of the Puerto Rican identity and a source of cultural pride on the island and abroad.

My Moon Within

Use this calendar to track the cycles of your body and heart with the cycle of the moon. This can be started at any time and used every month. Use this diagram to copy into your own monthly moon journal. Important: you do not need to menstruate to see how the moon affects you!

To begin, find the phase of the moon in the sky and mark that as your first day. Quiet your mind and think about what is happening inside of you. Use the spaces (see sample) to fill in a word(s) or symbol(s) to show how your body and heart feel on that day. Be as creative as you'd like! Repeat the following day until you've filled the entire month. Then, repeat the next month.

On the beautiful day your moon cycle arrives, make a new chart. Look to find where the moon is and mark that as your first day. Your moon might land on a waxing moon or a last quarter moon. This is okay! Start there and keep going throughout your cycle. The important thing is to find your connection to the celestial moon, to see what sort of dance you and Luna create!